The Day the MOUNTAIN Moved

RENNIE McOWAN

SAINT ANDREW PRESS

EDINBURGH

031948

First published in 1994 by
SAINT ANDREW PRESS
121 George Street, Edinburgh EH2 4YN

Copyright © Rennie McOwan 1994

ISBN 0 7152 0688 5

British Library Cataloguing in Publication Data
A catalogue record for this book
is available from the British Library.

ISBN 0715206885

Typeset in 11.5/13 pt Garamond.
Cover Illustration by Carrie Philip.
Cover concept by Mark Blackadder.
Printed in Great Britain by Bell and Bain Ltd, Glasgow.

Contents

Author's Note

THE children in this book, Gavin and his friends Clare, Michael and Mot, first appeared in *Light on Dumyat* (Saint Andrew Press, 1982) and *The White Stag Adventure* (Richard Drew Publishing Ltd, 1986; Saint Andrew Press 1992). Mot is actually Tom, but as a very young boy he wrote his name backwards and it stuck as a nickname.

Light on Dumyat was chosen for Central Region's primary schools conference at the University of Stirling. *The White Stag Adventure* was broadcast by the BBC for schools.

List of Pronunciations

Aluinn	=	Awe - leen
Beinn Venue	=	Ben Venoo
Cailleach Bheur	=	Cal - yach Vare
Dumyat	=	Dum - eye - at
Eoghann	=	Yaw - awn
Fianne	=	Fee - on
Fionn	=	Feen
Naoise	=	Noysha
Ossian	=	Aw - sheen
Tormud	=	Torramud
Uisneach	=	Oosh - nee - ach
Balquhidder	=	Balwhidder
feileadh beag	=	fail - ug bake
feileadh mor	=	fail - ug more
geas	=	guess
grianan	=	gree - annan
ptarmigan	=	tarmigan
sithich	=	shee - ich

For
Margaret Finn
~ with gratitude ~

CHAPTER I

The Moving Stone

GAVIN could hardly believe his eyes. The stone had moved. He was sure of it. He rubbed his eyes and looked again. The big, gray boulder perched on the side of a steep, grassy mound shook a little and then moved sideways and back again.

Gavin let out a gasp and then stopped and wiped his eyes.

He had been peering through an ancient piece of deer antler into which three holes had been cut, like panes of glass in an old window, and his eyes had been switching from one gap to the other.

He looked across the room at his friends: Clare, their leader, the ever dependable Michael and his younger brother Mot (who was really called Tom, but who as a small boy had written his name backwards and it had stuck ever since as a nickname).

Clare was lying on a couch on her back, humming tunelessly. She was bored. It had been raining all day and was only now starting to clear. Michael was whittling away at an old piece of wood he had found, trying to carve it into the head of a peregrine falcon, his favourite bird. Mot was reading an adventure story.

'Clare!' whispered Gavin. 'Come and have a look at this!'

'What is it?' said Clare, not bothering to get up. She glanced over and saw Gavin with the piece of deer antler.

'What's that you've got? Where did you get it?'

'I found it in an old chest in the cellar,' said Gavin. 'I was just poking around while it was raining outside, and I pulled back some boxes and there was a trunk or chest made of leather.

'It looked very old and battered. It's quite big too, and heavy.

1

I opened it and found this. There was nothing else. It's a bit dark down there, but I didn't see anything more.'

Clare got up and sauntered over. 'Let's have a look then,' she said and examined the antler.

It looked very old, dark brown and almost black in places, and yet where there were pale patches they looked very white, almost like patches on some plants which are about to die.

'What on earth is it?' she said, turning it over and over. 'What are the holes for?'

She peered through them at Gavin, and then stopped because her eyes began to water. 'Why three holes?' she commented. 'Why not just one? I wonder what it was for? I mean, it's not a natural hole. Someone has deliberately bored it.'

Gavin took it back from her and then caught her arm and pointed out of the window. 'See that boulder?' he asked. 'Well, look at it through the holes in this antler.'

Clare peered out. Just beyond the farmhouse was a long slope of the mountain called Ben Ledi, not far from the town of Callander. At the bottom of the slope was a grassy knoll or mound. Most of the mountain was still covered in swirling grey cloud and mist, and the grass and heather outside the window was shiny and wet with moisture after the heavy rain. She could see the hill burns, roaring down, white, brown and cream after days of storm.

The sun began to break through, sending long rays of light on to the wet hillside, great yellow streaks against a black and purple sky.

Clare found herself admiring the colours when Gavin pulled at her arm again. 'The boulder!' he exclaimed. 'The boulder! Look at the boulder!'

Clare examined the slope and saw the large boulder perched high on it. 'Okay, I see it. So, what now?'

Gavin began to hop up and down with impatience. 'Look at it through the holes in the antler! Go on! Look!'

Clare picked up the antler and peered through the three holes. For a moment she only saw the green and tawny hillside. Then she picked out the boulder, this time clearly seen in the sunlight and against the sky.

She looked at it in turn through the three holes and then she dropped the piece of antler. She gave a little exclamation of surprise. 'It moved!'

'I know,' said Gavin. 'It did that with me as well. It sort of trembled and shook and then moved sideways and back.'

Clare tried again. 'It might be that the three holes play tricks with the eyesight. Let's have another look.' She peered again, her brow frowning with concentration. 'Good grief!' she said. 'It moved again! *You* try!'

Gavin picked it up again and craned forward, taking his time and looking through each hole on their own and then once more together. He gave a little whistle. 'There's no doubt about it,' he said. 'The thing moves when you look at it through these holes. Let's get the others to try it.'

'Em ... no,' said Clare, cautiously. 'Let's have a look at that chest first. There may be other things in the cellar. Then I think we should hold a conference about what to do about it.'

Gavin nodded. He liked Clare's conferences and the way she made brisk, firm plans. She loved passwords and badges and special ceremonies.

They had had lots of adventures on other holidays they had been on together on a peak called Dumyat at the west end of the hills called the Ochils. There was also the time they protected a white stag. Some evil men were trying to capture it for a private zoo overseas.

Clare, Michael, Mot and Gavin had formed a gang which they called a Clan.

Clare walked over to Mot and Michael and gave both of them a friendly kick. She cut short their protests by saying: 'Come on, you two, we've got major business to attend to.'

The boys could see by her face and Gavin's that something important had happened.

'What's up?' asked Michael. 'What's the fuss about?'

Mot chipped in: 'Yes, what's going on. I was at an exciting bit in my story.'

'Never mind your stories,' said Clare. 'We may have a *real* adventure on our hands.

'We're going down to the cellar. Gavin's found an old chest and an odd piece of deer antler, and there may be other things.'

'What other things?' asked Michael.

'Yes,' added Mot. 'What's so exciting about an old piece of deer antler? Where is it anyway?'

Clare waved her hand. 'Oh, come on!' she said impatiently. 'You'll see in plenty of time. Gavin's got the antler, but leave it be just now.'

Gavin waved the piece of antler in the air, but before the boys could snatch it away Clare stepped in. When she was in that mood, the boys always gave in. She was their leader.

'The antler can wait,' she stressed. 'There may be something else very odd in that cellar, and if there is we've got to find out what it is.'

She opened a door and paused at the top of a flight of steep steps going down into a dark, narrow passage. 'Come on,' she said. 'Stop dawdling.'

The boys trooped after her along the passage and she turned through a narrow doorway, stooping as she did so. The old farmhouse had been built on the foundations of another, even older building and Clare's Uncle Fergus had told her that it may have been a kind of castle long ago.

She stopped and looked at the rough, old walls. She had done that many times since they had arrived there on holiday and Uncle Fergus had pointed the old cellar out to them when he took them round his new farm.

The doorway was small and narrow and there was a large

4

stone above the door, a lintel stone Uncle Fergus had called it. Electrical wiring had been put into the house, but in the cellar it was dim. Light only came from one bulb in the corridor.

Clare went into the small room, heaped high with old boxes, trunks, and farm tools from long ago, spades and forks and pieces of old iron.

'Which one was it?' she asked Gavin.

'That one,' he said. 'In that alcove.'

There was a stone hollow in one corner of the walls and it was easy to miss in the half-dark because it was covered in dust and cobwebs. Clare peered at the corner and made out the lines of a leather chest. She poked it and clouds of dust went up. It seemed to be quite heavy.

'Give me a hand,' she said, and the boys helped to tug it out into the middle of the room.

'The lid lifts up quite easily,' said Gavin. 'There were iron hooks or fastenings on the front. And when I pulled these up the lid opened no bother at all. I think it's a wooden chest inside a leather covering.'

Clare prodded it. It did seem hard. It seemed surprisingly big too, and it was heavy.

'Was the deer antler the only thing in it?' she asked Gavin.

'Yes,' he said. 'Mind you, I only had a quick look because there was so much dust flying around.'

Clare looked at the chest thoughtfully. It certainly looked very old and seemed to have been there for years.

'Right!' she said. 'Let's have another look.'

She leaned forward and lifted the lid.

CHAPTER II
The Prophecy

CLOUDS of dust filled the room and set the boys coughing.

'I can hardly see in here,' spluttered Clare, putting her arms into the chest and slowly feeling her way around. 'I can't see or feel anything else. Wait a minute, though! There *is* something else here! Some kind of metal clasp or catch inside as well as outside.'

She fiddled around inside while the boys looked on. They all began to feel slightly uneasy.

'I'm not sure I like this,' said Michael.

'Me, neither,' agreed Mot.

'Oh, don't be such babies,' said Clare. 'If you don't explore things then you find nothing. After all, Gavin found a piece of deer antler.'

'What's so important about that?' asked Mot. 'Just a silly old piece of antler.'

'It's anything but silly!' retorted Clare. 'You'll see in a minute—won't they, Gavin?'

'Yes ... sure,' said Gavin, almost wishing at that point that he hadn't opened the chest.

'But what's so special about the antler, Gavin?' persisted Michael.

Clare cut in again. 'Don't ask so many questions. Oh, I can't see in here. Michael, go and get a torch. There's something at the side of the chest. I can feel it, but I can't see it.'

Michael left the room and soon returned with a little head torch, the kind mountaineers use on the hills. It had a strap round it so it could be worn on the head, like a miner's lamp. On the hills, this allows the climber's arms to remain free. The battery sits at the back of the head.

He switched it on and a satisfying beam of light cut through the dust-filled air and showed the chest clearly.

'That's better!' said Clare. 'Put the light on to the chest and inside.'

Michael leaned forward, and Gavin and Mot hovered on the fringes.

'Ah!' said Clare. 'It's got some kind of hinge or catch. Just a minute and I'll try and get it to move.' She grasped the little iron catch between her fingers, pushing it gently in all directions.

Suddenly there was a little click and the bottom of the chest sprang up a little. Clare stood back and looked at it.

'What is it?' asked Michael.

'Yes, come on Clare, tell us what it is,' said Mot. 'Don't leave us in the dark.'

'Well, come closer and you won't be in the dark,' said Clare, and she gestured for the boys to come forward. 'It's got a false bottom or floor,' she said. 'Hold on a minute and I'll try and lift it up.'

She leaned over and got her fingers round the edge of what seemed to be wooden board covered in thick leather or deer skin. She pulled it out and examined it. 'Bring that torch nearer,' she said. She tapped the board with her hand and more dust fell off and swirled around. Again they all began to cough.

'Let's get it out of here,' she said, 'and have a proper look at it.'

'Good idea!' said Michael. 'Do you realise this means I'm going to have to wash *twice* in the one day?'

'Some days you don't wash at all, or you wouldn't if you could get away with it,' retorted Clare. She took one end of the board and motioned to Gavin to take the other.

'Shut the lid and put it back where it was, Mot,' she added. 'We'll have a look at this upstairs in my room where there's better light.'

Mot obediently shut the lid and closed the iron clasps or hasps into their slots on the outside of the chest and pushed it back into the alcove.

Michael shoved some of the old boxes and trunks back against the wall so that the alcove was hidden.

'We don't want the grown-ups in on all this yet,' he explained. 'Let's examine it in peace and quiet.'

They trooped upstairs to Clare's room, but it took all four of them to carry it easily. It was heavier than it looked.

Before going in, Clare called down to her Aunt Elspeth that they would be down soon for lunch. Their uncle and aunt were quite unusual for grown-ups. They let Clare, Gavin, Michael and Mot spend their holidays on the farm, and gave them a lot of freedom to wander and explore. The children had great fun.

Clare shut her bedroom door and they dumped the piece of wood on the floor. Gavin, Michael and Mot gathered round and they all gazed at it.

'There's a kind of stitching round the edge, Clare,' Michael pointed out.

'So there is,' said Mot, examining it closely.

Sure enough, the edges of what seemed to be deer skin were pinned together by large but neat stitches, using a kind of thick lace or thong as thread.

Clare fingered them. 'They're very firm and tight,' she said. 'Whoever did that knew what they were doing. Take an end, Gavin, and we'll turn it over. It's quite heavy.'

Gavin took hold of one end of the board and Clare took the other and, just to get in on the act, Michael and Mot took one side and together they heaved it over.

'One end is open,' said Clare. 'Look! It's like the open end of a bag.'

'So it is,' said Gavin. 'Grab an end, Clare, and I'll try and slide the bag off the board.'

They each took corners and tugged and pulled. More dust

flew up until the wooden board began to emerge from the deer skin bag. It was brown and dark and clearly very old.

'Look!' said Mot, who was closest to that part of the board. 'It's got lettering on it.'

'So it has,' said Clare. 'What next!?'

They pulled the deer skin bag totally off and placed it in a corner of the room and examined the board again. It was about four feet long, two feet wide, about three inches deep—and although the surface was dusty, the bag had kept it free from most dirt. Clare went to her drawer, took out a handkerchief and wiped at the board until some of the dust came off.

The boys could make out some lettering, but not much. Clare had to soak her handkerchief under the tap and scrub hard at the board before it all became clear.

'It's a poem,' said Clare. 'Look, it's a whole lot of lines set out like a poem.'

The boys examined it closely.

'Or is it a wish of some kind?' asked Gavin. 'It's like a verse set out like a wish.'

'It might be a prophecy,' said Michael. 'It's something special anyway, otherwise who would take the trouble to carve it out like that and then wrap it up.'

Clare began to read the first line. It was carved in deep letters with little curves at the corners, some of which had broken off. She found herself hesitating every now and again because she couldn't make out all the words.

'You ... must find ... the ... hidden spring ... ,' she read and then stopped.

'Go on, go on!' said Michael, excitedly. 'Don't stop.'

'I can't make it all out,' said Clare, rubbing away at the letters with her handkerchief. 'That's better. We'll need to be careful. This wood is starting to crumble.'

She read the next line: 'You must hear the harper sing .... Well, what does that mean?'

The boys looked puzzled.

'Read the lot, all the way through,' said Gavin. 'Then we can perhaps guess at it. It's hard when you're just doing bits of it.'

'Okay,' said Clare. 'Here goes.' Occasionally hesitating at some words because the wood had crumbled and continued to break up as she held the edge of it, she read:

> 'You must find the hidden spring,
> You must hear the harper sing,
> You must hear the cuckoo call,
> You must find the golden wall,
> You must blow the magic horn,
> You must find the maid forlorn,
> You must climb the sacred hill,
> You must see the dogs that kill,
> You must seek the hidden tree,
> or lost forever you will be.'

She stopped at the end and a silence fell on them all. It all seemed eery and fey and a little bit frightening.

The boys said nothing and then Clare read it again, this time more slowly and clearly.

'What do you make of that?' she asked.

'Dunno,' said Michael. 'It's magic of some kind, I think, but I don't know what. Perhaps it's a magic rhyme.'

'It has a kind of ring to it,' said Clare, and read it for a third time while the boys listened.

Gavin took a little notebook from his pocket and wrote the words down. He was a great believer in his notebooks.

'Do you think it has anything to do with your antler, Gavin?' she asked.

'I don't know,' said Gavin.

'Yes, and what about that antler?' asked Mot.

'Yes, what about it?' added Michael. 'What have you two been up to, anyway? Why didn't you tell us about it. What took you to the chest? There's something been going on this morning, Clare. Why didn't you and Gavin tell us about it?'

Clare began to look annoyed, so Gavin said hurriedly: 'It was me, Michael. I found a piece of antler in the chest and it has three holes cut in it. Something odd happened to me with it this morning, but I didn't want to look a fool. I told Clare and then all of us went down to the cellar to look at the chest.'

Mot chimed in: 'But *what's* so special about your antler?'

'You'll see,' said Clare. 'If you think this board is odd, wait until you see the boulder?'

'What boulder?' asked Mot, in a tone of exasperation.

'The one on the shoulder of Ben Ledi—the one you can see from the front window,' said Gavin.

'Oh, that one,' said Michael. 'Uncle Fergus told me about that. It's just a boulder left by the glacier when the ice moved on. Grown-ups call it an erratic. Uncle Fergus said that the people long ago believed that two giants had a contest and one of them flung the boulder there.'

'Well, come and see,' said Clare. 'Gavin, bring your antler and we'll show them what happens.' She added, with a touch of seriousness in her voice, 'Watch carefully—the boulder moves if you look at it.'

Michael jeered: 'A boulder that moves!? Pull the other one!'

'It *does* move!' insisted Gavin. 'It moved for Clare and I when we looked at it through the antler holes.'

'I'll bet!' said Mot sarcastically. 'Any minute now we'll have flying deer and walking fish!'

Clare stalked towards the door. 'Leave the board here,' she said. 'Come on, you two. We'll show you!'

Gavin walked towards the door, carrying his piece of antler. He turned to Mot and Michael and said, with a slight catch in his voice, 'It *does* move! You'll see!'

CHAPTER III

The Storm

GAVIN went over to the window and pointed outside. The sun was now shining brightly and the big boulder on the slopes of Ben Ledi sparkled in the light. 'There it is!' he said.

'Well, what's so special about it,' asked Michael, gazing at the hillside.

'Yes, what's so special,' said Mot, who had the habit of sounding like an echo.

Clare's voice took on her leader tone. 'Gavin! Give them the antler.' Gavin handed the antler to Michael.

'Look at the boulder through the holes,' he said.

Michael did so and, like Clare before him, he dropped the antler on the floor. 'It *moved!*' he breathed. 'It shook, then moved sideways.'

'Oh, rubbish!' commented Mot. 'Let me have a look. It's all a trick of the light, or raindrops on the outside of the window, something like that.'

He picked up the antler and looked through it, trying each hole in turn and closing one eye like a man with a telescope. He then held it in front of him and tried squinting through all three holes at the same time.

There was an awed silence. 'You know, you're right,' said Mot, with feeling. 'It *does* move.'

Clare thought for a bit: 'Let's all look through the window in turn without the antler and see if anything happens.'

'Good idea!' said Gavin, so they all did that. The boulder remained firmly rooted to the hillside.

'Now, all together with the antler in turn,' said Clare. 'I'll start —I'm the leader.'

'Fine,' said Mot, making a face at Clare behind her back and quickly switching it to a grin when she turned round and glared at him.

She looked through the holes and muttered: 'Yes, it moved again, but this time it sort of trembled and then moved the other way and then back again.'

Gavin took the second look. The same thing happened. He began to feel excitement building up inside him. It was as if they were waking some kind of sleeping beast.

Michael took his turn and said: 'Yes, there's no mistake about it. It moved, and it shifted the other way this time. What on earth is going on? Here you are, Mot.'

Mot, well accustomed as the youngest to getting the last turn at anything, took the antler and gazed through the holes. 'Yes, it's moving,' he said, in the manner of a TV or radio broadcaster commenting on a football match. 'Yes, it has shaken about a bit. Yes, it's moving to the right .... ' Then his tone changed to one of near alarm. 'Now it's moving back to the left .... It didn't do that last time. It's shaking itself all about. I don't like this. I think we should stop.'

At that moment there was a blinding flash and a great roaring noise began. A wind sprang up, as in a storm, and began to howl and wail. The house shook and the children clung to one another as the shaking became more marked and the noise grew louder.

The house filled with a white mist which, snake-like, began to coil around them until they could no longer see one another. It was like being lost in a snow storm when everything is white and there is no sky, no ground, just endless whiteness and the roaring wind.

Their senses began to reel and the children clung to pieces of furniture while the storm raged and shrieked and the whiteness grew until they could no longer see and they lost all sense of time and place.

Amid the fury, the piece of antler was dropped on the floor. It, too, was soon covered up by the white mist.

The children no longer knew *who* they were or *where* they were. They felt themselves soaring, as if through the sky, while all around them the white storm raged and the roaring continued like the bellowing of some maddened animal.

Suddenly, all went quiet.

CHAPTER IV

Lost forever

CLARE was the first to get her wits back. She was sitting on the hillside where the boulder had been, but now there was no boulder, just grass and heather, wild and rough.

Gavin, Michael and Mot lay nearby and after a few minutes they began to stir and sit up.

'What was all that about?' she muttered as she gazed around. She could make out the boys easily enough, but she was puzzled —there was something strange about them.

'Clare!' asked Michael. 'Are you okay?'

'Yes,' said Clare. 'Just a bit battered. What happened?'

'I don't know,' said Gavin. Then he stopped and said in great surprise: 'Clare, you're *dressed* differently.'

Clare looked down at herself. 'So I am!' Then she looked at the boys. 'So are *you*! You've all got a kind of kilt on.'

The boys looked at themselves, confused and a little alarmed. They were wearing a kilt of tartan, but not like the sort of kilt people wear today. It was as if another half had been added so that the kilt went round the waist and then up round the shoulders —something like a shawl, or the kind of plaid pipers wear. It was pinned high up with a silver brooch carved into a series of intricate whorls and twisting lines, running into one another.

The back of the kilts had pleats, big ones made up of folds in the cloth and not stitched together. They had long sleeved shirts on and a kind of blue bonnet on their heads, like the balmorals they used to wear when they had their Clan Alliance during other holidays. Their hair was longer and roughly cut.

'Clare!' asked Michael. 'Are you okay?'
'Yes,' said Clare. 'Just a bit battered. What happened?'

They continued to examine themselves in bewilderment. Each boy had a leather belt around his waist and a kind of bag, or sporran, not hung at the front as nowadays, but worn on the hip and attached to the belt. The hem of the kilt was much higher than that worn today and their legs were tanned a deep brown as if by the sun. On their feet they had shoes made of deer hide with little holes cut in the top parts.

Clare's brothers were struck dumb, but Gavin said: 'Look at yourself, Clare.'

They all turned and looked at Clare. For once, she was silent. She was wearing a green dress made of some kind of linen which had been dyed, with cuffs and a belt made of rich material— gold, red, blue and yellow—which contrasted with the green dress.

Her hem had the same kind of material on it and she wore a headband of what looked like gold. Her hair was long and hung down her back.

She, too, wore shoes of deer hide, but hers were ornamented with colourful embroidery patterns, circles and whorls. The tips of her laces looked as if they had been finished off with silver.

'You look like a princess, Clare,' gasped Michael, awestruck.

'Well, what are we?' asked Gavin, examining his kilt and sporran. 'What are we? Are we Clare's servants?'

'Why not? Nothing changes ... ,' grumbled Mot with a wan smile. He was beginning to find all this too much for him.

'I must say you look very nice, Clare,' said Gavin.

'Oh, don't give her any airs,' said Michael. 'Well, any ideas? What has happened to us? What did we do? Did we cause the storm or was it the boulder? And where's the antler?'

Clare found her voice. 'It must have been the boulder. That old piece of antler must have worked some kind of spell. What it's all about, I've no idea? We'd better try and get back to the farm.'

'What farm?' said Gavin. 'I don't see the farm.' He gazed

around. Then he got the second major shock of the day. 'Clare! The landscape's all changed.'

'No, it hasn't,' said Michael. 'There's Ben Ledi. It's disappearing into the mist every now and again, but it's the same mountain as before.'

'But things have changed,' said Mot. 'Where's Callander? It's gone. There's nothing where it was before.'

'Yes,' said Gavin looking around. 'It *is* different. Where are the roads ... houses ... telephone wires?'

The children gazed around from the knoll where the boulder had once sat and saw a different countryside. It was almost the same and yet it was different.

The grass and heather was longer, all the houses had gone, there were no roads, and where Callander and the farmhouse had been there was now only miles of woodland, much of which grew high up the hillsides. It looked beautiful in the sun which by now was dispersing the mist; but it also looked wild and lonely.

'You know what I think?' said Clare.

'What?' the boys chorused.

Occasionally Clare used a tone which meant she was saying something very important. She was usually right. 'I think we've started some kind of spell with the antler and the boulder. We've taken ourselves back in time ... very far back, I think. Look at all the trees. Uncle Fergus told me that, long ago, when there were far fewer deer and hardly any sheep, trees and woods grew all over the place, even quite far up the hillsides.'

'That's right!' agreed Gavin, the collector of information. Without thinking, he opened his sporran and took out his notebook. There was a chorus of surprise. It seemed to be the only thing from the present which they still had with them.

Gavin flicked over a page. 'Uncle Fergus told me that one of the old names for Scotland was Caledonia. The Romans called it that. It is supposed to come from words which mean the wooded stronghold.'

He closed his notebook and put it back in his sporran.

'Oh, wonderful!' said Clare, sarcastically. 'That's a great help. Have you any information that will get us back to modern times again? Where's the antler, by the way? It helped to get us here. Perhaps it can help get us back.'

There was silence. 'It must have been dropped when the storm and all that noise broke out,' said Michael. 'We've left it behind.'

'That's all we need,' said Clare. 'Stuck thousands of years in the past with no means of getting back.'

Gavin took out his notebook again. 'But remember, we've got the prophecy, the one that was on the board. Perhaps it will help us. I copied it out in my notebook.'

Clare's tone softened. 'Good man!' she said. 'That old notebook of yours will prove useful yet. Let's have a look.'

She took the notebook and slowly read the poem again. She shook her head in puzzlement. 'We could try and do *all* these things, but we don't know what they mean.'

Michael chipped in: 'And even if we *did* know, we can't be sure it would help take us back.'

Clare began to assume an air of command. 'Well, there's no sense in standing here moping. We have to do something. Let's see what we have between us in the way of food or equipment or other clothes.'

They delved into their sporrans again, which were quite big, and inside found little bags of deer skin which held oatmeal. Clare stuck her finger inside a bag and then licked it. 'Yeuch!' she said. 'It's tasteless ... like cardboard. What on earth have we got that for? We've nothing to cook it with anyway.'

Gavin pulled out his notebook again:

'Uncle Fergus told me something about that,' he said. The rest looked at him with a mixture of exasperation and amusement. Gavin's notebook was always filled with bits of information and details of interesting birds he had seen or plants or stones he had found.

'Oh, you can laugh,' he said, 'but Uncle Fergus told me that oatmeal was a campaign food in the days of the clans. It was a kind of emergency ration. They took a handful and mixed it up with a little water and then ate it. It was called *dramach*.'

'What did they mix it in?' asked Mot. 'We don't have any bowls or spoons.'

'Well,' said Gavin, hesitating slightly. 'They sometimes stirred it up in the heel of their shoes.'

'What!' said Michael. He made a sick face and muttered, 'Ugh, disgusting!'

'It's not as bad as it sounds, Clare,' said Mot. 'They probably washed the shoe out first. The heel part inside the shoe does form a little hollow if you tilt it up a little. You can always stir it with a stick. Their shoes were called *currans*.'

'Oh, brilliant!' said Clare, again with sarcasm. 'We're stuck with only a handful of old porridge to eat.' Then she laughed.

Gavin smiled. That was more like the old Clare. She wasn't given to complaining, but to making decisions and to solving problems and having fun.

'At least we have some kind of food for a few hours anyway,' she said. 'But we've got to find some kind of shelter while we figure out what we're going to do. We could make a hut.'

The Clan were very good at making huts and they were on the point of deciding to do that in the woods that stretched out in all directions, when Mot had a better idea.

'Look,' he said. 'There's a huge huddle of boulders and rocks on that hillside. There are bound to be caves or hollows where we could build up a sheltering wall with turf and stones. That's a better idea. There's also a burn there where we can get water.'

'And where we can stir up the dramach,' added Michael.

They all laughed and felt better.

The children tramped through the woods, beginning to enjoy the feel of turf and heather beneath their deer skin shoes. It was soft and relaxing and made them feel nimble. If they came to wet bits, the water ran out of the holes again and their feet soon warmed up.

'This spell must have made us tougher,' said Clare. 'It's quite cold but we're not feeling it, and you boys all have long, tanned legs. These clothes seem to be made of wool and that can be very warm.'

Indeed, they all felt very fit. Even though Clare looked like a princess in her green dress and her golden headband, she too looked tanned and fresh as if she had spent most of her life out of doors. It was as if the spell had taken them back and then ensured that they would be able to cope with bad weather without suffering or becoming ill.

Every now and again Gavin went over to a tree and broke off any dead branches. 'We might need these for a fire,' he said.

'We don't have any matches,' commented Michael.

Gavin's face fell. 'Never mind. We might manage to get some kind of spark.' He kept collecting wood, but not from the ground where it is always damp and no good for kindling. He concentrated on birch and rowan trees whose dead twigs burn easily. Soon he had a little bundle which he tucked under his arm.

'Not far now,' said Clare as they walked up a little brae to the big huddle of boulders. They could see the sun shining on the waters of a loch in the distance and the landscape shone and seemed welcoming.

They began to cheer up and Gavin hummed a little song. But it didn't come out the way he wanted it to. It was as if there was some mechanism inside him which told him to do certain things, so that his tune turned out to be like a pipe tune, like a march. Nevertheless, he sang quite happily and was amazed to find that Clare, Michael and Mot all joined in the harmony. They seemed to know his song as well.

'Goodness,' Gavin thought. 'I may be somewhere back in time with no idea how to get back, but I'm beginning to enjoy this adventure. How odd.'

They began to poke around the boulders, clambering over them and peering into hollows looking for a suitable cave. There were plenty of holes, but none big enough to take all four of them, and which were also dry. Twice they went into big caves only to come hurrying back out because a dead deer or wild goat lay inside, animals which had probably sought shelter when ill or wounded by hunters.

Mot began to climb higher up the hill. He disappeared for a bit and then reappeared and shouted down: 'Come up here. There's a big cave and it's dry. It runs quite far back.'

They began to climb up to him, occasionally teetering on the top of large stones which moved, or clambering from one boulder to another. Then they all stopped, startled. From up above, they heard Mot shout.

They looked up at him. They could see him clearly, his reddish-brown tartan standing out against the grey rocks. He began to hurry down to them leaping from stone to stone like a goat. Gavin looked at him with amazement.

Mot stopped suddenly just short of them. Before they could speak, he raised his hand and arm as if *demanding* silence. They were so taken aback that their excited questions stopped and even Clare was struck dumb.

'Clare!' hissed Mot, 'There's someone in the cave!'

CHAPTER V

The Night of the Harp

'WHO is it ... did they see you?' asked Clare as they quickly dodged behind the boulders. The Clan were good at becoming invisible out of doors when they wanted to be.

'No, he didn't see me,' whispered Mot. 'There's a small entrance, and then when you go in the cave takes a kind of twist and opens out into quite a big cave. I was just thinking it would suit us fine when I saw something in the corner.

'I thought it was perhaps another dead deer or goat and then I saw it was a man. He was lying down, sound asleep, wrapped in a kind of tartan cloak, a bit like ours. I watched him for a bit because the light wasn't very good. When I saw he had a huge sword, I thought I'd better leave.'

Clare looked anxious: 'A sword? I don't like the sound of that. Did he look like a bandit? Was he alone?'

'How could I tell whether he was a bandit or not,' retorted Mot. 'I could hardly see him. But he *was* on his own. He seemed to have a kind of bundle beside him, but I couldn't see more than that.'

Clare pondered for a moment, then said: 'Let's all go and take a look. We're in a drastic situation which requires drastic action. He's hardly likely to harm four children, but we'd better have a plan. If he turns nasty then we all run for it in four different directions.'

She gazed around. At the edge of the wood below them were two large boulders, covered in moss and lichen at the tops and fringed by a little grove of birches.

'See these stones?' Clare asked.

The boys followed her pointing hand and nodded.

'Well, if we have to scatter, that will be the point where we meet up again later. Let's hope we don't have to.'

She led the way uphill, closely followed by Mot, with Michael and Gavin keeping slightly to the side. Nearer the cave mouth she signalled for Michael and Gavin to go to one side and she and Mot went to the other.

'I'll go in first,' she said, keeping her voice low. 'I'm the leader. If I shout "run for it" then scatter in different directions. Is that clear?'

'Yes,' said Michael. 'But I'm not happy about you taking the risks on your own. Let's all go in together.'

'There isn't room for that,' said Mot. 'But we could keep very close to Clare.'

'Okay,' said Michael. 'Lead on, Clare.'

She tip-toed into the cave entrance, closely followed by Michael and the others. The cave took a little twist, just as Mot said, and then opened out into a kind of cavern. Enough light came in to allow her a glimpse of a man lying on his side at the far end of the cave.

They spread out inside the entrance and stood there silently. To their astonishment the man rolled over, sat up and looked steadily at them.

They all took a step backward and were ready to run when he said: 'Don't be afraid. I heard the first of you come in and I thought there would be more.'

He gave a smile and Clare relaxed a little. He was not a big man, but small and wiry. He had very fair hair and Clare noticed that it seemed to grow low down on his forehead as well as over the rest of his head.

He stood up and dusted himself down. He was wearing a tartan plaid in colours which were mainly blue and green. Instead of the kilts the boys were wearing he wore tartan trousers, shaped like tights which were close to the line of his legs and calves. He had deer hide shoes on his feet. Like Clare's, they were ornamented at the end of each lace or thong.

A huge golden brooch pinned the corner of his plaid and he had a kind of leather thong around his neck and shoulder. From that hung a great sword, almost big enough for two men to swing.

Beside him was a kind of sack, made of skin.

'Who are you?' asked Clare.

The man studied them. Then he said in a clear, steady voice like someone making an announcement: 'I am Ossian, son of the great god, Fionn, and I am on my way to collect my favourite hound, Bran. I am a poet and a bard. This is my *clarsach*.'

He reached round behind him and took a little harp out of the deer skin bag. He brushed it with his fingers and the strings made a lovely, rippling noise, like water gurgling in a burn, or a quiet wind sighing through the trees. It was a soothing noise and the children relaxed.

Ossian looked at them gravely. He held his hand up in a kind of salute, like Red Indians in Westerns. As he looked at Gavin, Michael and Mot in turn, each found themselves raising their hand in the same salute.

When he looked at Clare he made a deep bow and, almost without thinking, she gave a kind of slight curtsey. It seemed both an odd and normal thing to do in the circumstances.

'Where are you going, princess?' he asked. 'And why are you travelling with such young men as your guards?'

'I'm not a princess,' said Clare.

Gavin, Michael and Mot, pleased at being called young men, all began to speak at once until Ossian held his hand up again and called for silence.

'Sit down,' he commanded. 'Tell me who you are and where you are going.'

They sat down beside him on the dry floor of the cave. As Clare told their story, Ossian strummed on his harp every now and again. Twice, when Clare came to dramatic bits, he struck the strings in a loud chord.

His face grew still as the tale unfolded. He began to look very grave, but he stayed silent until Clare had finished talking.

'I see,' he said, brushing his fair hair back. Again the children could see that it grew very low on his forehead.

'Where is the antler now?' he asked.

'We lost it in the storm, when the stone moved,' said Clare.

Ossian grew excited: 'I can say that it was a special antler. It belonged to a great, white stag long ago and my people kept it in the special lands where all beautiful people dwell—The Land Beyond The Sunset, The Land Under The Waves and The Land Of The Ever Young. We had three holes cut in it because three is a magic number.'

The children were silent as they watched his face and heard his voice explain their mystery to them: 'The antler must have passed from my people to the people who built their castle on the mound close to your farm. Then it was lost and was hidden for centuries until the new races found it. They would not know what it was, so they would put it away and forget about it.

'The boulder, too, was special to us, but we could not move it and get back into The Land Beneath The Mountains unless we had the antler. You found it and now you have been taken back through centuries until my time.'

He turned to Clare. 'Are you their leader?' he asked.

Clare nodded, bemused by such dramatic news.

'That is why you have been dressed like a princess,' said Ossian. 'Your brothers and your friend have been made your attendants and warriors.'

He turned to the boys: 'Guard her well!' he said. 'It is only by all surviving together that you will return to your home again. Give me the prophecy you told me about.'

Gavin took out his notebook and read the poem out loud.

Ossian listened intently and said: 'Yes, much of our old magic is still here and if you fulfill all of these things you will get back home. But beware! This earth is full of evil beings who will want to enslave you all and keep you here. Trust no one until you are sure they are ready to help you.'

He smiled at Gavin: 'If the storm had continued longer, your book would have been destroyed like all your old clothing. You are fortunate indeed.'

He reached into his sack and took out a fistful of feathers. He gave them to Clare, saying, 'These belong to the bird called the ptarmigan. It lives high in the hills and its feathers are very white in the winter. When time began it was the mother bird of all other birds and it is very special to me and to all the other gods of the hills.

'If you are in trouble, tap your heart three times with the feathers and they will protect you.'

Clare put the feathers away safely in a little pouch attached to her belt.

Gavin chipped in: 'Ossian ... sir,' he began. He didn't mean to start like that but it seemed fitting and good mannered to be formal, particularly when talking to a kind of god. 'Might I ask you a question?'

Ossian nodded gravely, but a little smile played around his lips as he looked at the Clan gathered at his feet.

'Where do we go to fulfil the prophecy?' Gavin asked. 'Where should we start? Can you tell us?'

'No, I cannot do that,' said Ossian. 'I do not know when and where you will meet these things. If I did, it would destroy the prophecy if I told you. You must wander and explore and be ready at all times.'

Michael looked up: 'Please tell us more about yourself, Ossian. Where did you come from and why are you helping us?'

Ossian paused for a moment, then said: 'My father is called Fionn and he is also called Fingal. He is a god and a warrior in the mountains. He has magic powers. We live in a land where there are witches and wizards, water sprites and banshees, a land of trees and hills and lochs, a land of great beauty—but a land where bad spirits as well as good spirits dwell.

'My father has many warriors at his command, but they are hidden and can only be summoned to his aid by magic.

'He is called Fionn because his hair is fair, like mine. He had a faery wife, but left her to marry a human being like yourselves.

'Well, my faery mother grew angry and changed my human mother into a deer. Thus, when I was born, my mother touched my forehead in the same way a mother deer licks her fawn, so my hair grew there as well.'

Gavin and the others listened to this strange tale with a mixture of emotions: relief at finding a friend, anxiety at being stuck centuries away from their real home, and fear at what might lie ahead of them.

'We need a plan,' said Clare. 'Before we can journey, we need some food and more clothing.'

Ossian leaned forward and handed Clare two pieces of stone. 'Strike these together and you will get sparks,' he said. 'Put very dry moss and heather together and light them with the sparks: always keep some dry material inside a little bag like mine.'

He pulled open his bag and put his hand inside and pulled out a little pouch, also made of skin. Inside was a little bundle of very dry grass and moss. 'Once you have that lit then you can build a fire,' he said. 'I'll show you how.'

He built a little fire on the floor at the entrance to the cave and then produced a small iron plate from his sack and put it on stones, over the flames. He began to cook some strips of deer meat on the iron plate.

The Clan watched with envy. Ossian smiled and then handed them morsels to eat until they all declared themselves satisfied.

'Now sleep!' he said. 'You must journey tomorrow and I have to leave you.'

He reached into his bag again and pulled out a long piece of tartan cloth like the kilt-and-plaid the boys wore and handed it to Clare. 'Wrap yourself in that,' he said. 'It is wool and very warm and comfortable.'

Gavin felt bold enough to ask further questions: 'What are these kilts we are wearing?' he asked. 'Why aren't we wearing short kilts?'

Ossian replied: 'That is what people wear in this time. The wool comes from their sheep, the dye from plants and leaves. They keep the tartan pattern of different colours of wool marked on sticks and weave it on small looms.

'Your garment is two pieces of tartan stitched together. It is called the *feileadh mor*, which is Gaelic for "big plaid". The kilt people wear in your time is called the *feileadh beag*, or "little kilt". It is not suitable for sleeping in.' Ossian smiled again. 'Now you know.'

Ossian wrapped himself in his plaid like a big blanket, curled up and went to sleep.

The Clan, worn out by the day's adventures, did the same. Soon the only sound in the cave was the steady deep breathing of sleeping people.

But, just before she dropped off, Clare suddenly shot upright and tugged at Ossian's arm. 'Wait a minute! *You're* the harper!' she cried. 'Why didn't I think of it before? You can be the harper in our prophecy. You *must* sing, Ossian! Please sing! Do it now and that will be our first step.'

The boys, awoken by her voice, were taken aback at her excitement. But Clare went on: 'The prophecy! The prophecy! It says "we must hear the harper sing". You're a bard, Ossian— please sing!'

Ossian smiled slowly. 'You are right. But I could not tell you that without spoiling the spell. You had to find out for yourselves. I did want you to, but I could not tell you. Very well, I'll sing for you, and with a glad heart.'

He picked up his clarsach and strummed on the strings while

he tightened them up. When he was satisfied they were in tune, he began to sing a gentle tune, like a lullaby, which told of white sands and blue seas, cool winds, murmuring burns and deep green woods, of shady hollows in the hills where the deer lay in warm sunlight. Gradually the children's eyes grew heavier and, one by one, they fell asleep.

Clare was the last to drop off. 'You must find the hidden spring,' she muttered to herself. 'That's the next one!' Still talking quietly to herself she fell asleep.

When they awoke in the morning Ossian had gone.

CHAPTER VI

The Grey Cloud

CLARE woke first. She wondered where she was for a time and then saw long shafts of sunlight striking the twisting walls of the cave entrance. For a moment she felt a pang of fear. What was going to happen to them?

Then she realised that her bed was not the hard floor of the cave, but a little 'mattress' of heather. She looked around and the boys were also lying on little piles of heather and were still asleep.

Ossian must have done it, she thought. Perhaps he had put some kind of spell on them to make them sleep deeply. Then she noticed that she was wrapped in a long belted plaid of the same kind as the boys wore and she felt very warm. She threw it off and straightened her dress and put her currans and gold headband back on. In a pocket she found a comb made of deer antler. That was a surprise. She hadn't noticed that before. She began to comb her long hair and felt better.

The boys also began to stir, making comments about their heather beds. 'Clare!' said Gavin. 'Ossian's given each of us a kind of rucksack and there's a knife and fork inside made of bone, and a spare tartan plaid.'

'Yes,' said Michael. 'The rucksacks have little straps, and we can wear them on our back. This deer skin is quite soft and it still has all the hair on the outside. Perhaps that's to let the rain run off it.'

Mot was closely examining his sack and noted that it had a kind of drawstring at the neck made of deer hide, which pulled it all together.

The boys protested noisily when Clare sent them outside the cave to a little burn so they could wash their faces and hands. They eventually went, keeping up their chorus of grumbling.

Clare picked up her sack and it felt surprisingly heavy. She raked around inside. As well as a bone knife and fork, she also pulled out a round, iron plate like the one Ossian had cooked on. It wasn't big, but it was heavy. She thought they might all have to take it in turns to carry it.

Then she found another two objects—a smaller bag inside the big one and a jar made of some kind of stoneware. It had a kind of cork made of wood stuck firmly in the neck.

Clare opened the small bag and inside were twelve cakes or scones which looked as if they had been made with some kind of barley. They were wrapped inside a clean piece of white linen which smelled very fresh when Clare picked it up and sniffed it.

'Things are looking up,' she thought. 'We've got breakfast and, if needs be, we have dramach if we have to travel. If we can get some meat we also have a plate to cook it on over a fire.'

The boys came back into the cave rubbing drops of water off their faces and hands, demanding that Clare inspect them to see how clean they were.

'No, thanks,' said Clare. 'Who would want to examine you three from close up?'

'Clare! We're starving,' said Michael. 'Do you think we should eat our dramach?'

'No,' said Clare. 'I've got something better.'

The boys stared at the cakes in front of them with little enthusiasm.

'What are they?' asked Michael, dubiously. 'Where did you get them?'

'Cakes or scones of some sort. They *are* good! I've tried one,' retorted Clare.

Mot picked one up and broke off a corner and ate it. 'Hey, it's not bad,' he agreed.

Gavin picked up one as well and thought it was rather like eating an oatcake.

'I've got something else as well,' said Clare. 'There's something in this jar. Ossian left the cakes and the jar for us. It's got some kind of cork in it made of wood, but I can't get it out.'

'Here, let me try,' said Gavin. He reached into his sack and pulled out the bone knife and inserted it at the base of the plug of wood and worked it around a little.

With a slight pop out came the plug. Clare put her finger into the jar and felt something stick. She licked her finger and then gave a beaming smile. 'It's honey,' she said. 'We can have some with our barley cakes. Are your hands clean?'

The boys, glad for once that they had washed, put out their hands like the dwarfs in Walt Disney's film 'Snow White'. Clare declared them clean enough to stick their fingers in the jar.

'We'd better be careful with this,' she said. 'It may have to last us a long time. You're only allowed two dips each.' She kept a close eye on the boys as they twice dipped a finger into the jar and sucked it. The cakes soon vanished.

They all sat back on the floor of the cave, enjoying the soft feeling of the extra tartan plaids beneath them like a kind of rug.

'We need a plan,' decided Clare. 'We've heard the magic harp sing so that should be the start of us getting back, but I've no idea where we find the rest, or even whether we're supposed to find them in order?'

'I know,' said Gavin. 'It's very difficult.'

Michael pondered for a moment: 'Why don't we head for that loch we saw in the distance. We might catch fish there, and if there are any people around then it's likely they'll live beside a place like that. They might even have boats.'

'But we don't know whether there *are* people,' said Mot. 'Ossian said he lived in a land of witches and banshees and good and bad spirits. He said nothing about people.'

'True,' said Clare. 'But we can't sit about doing nothing. The only way we can even try and do everything in the prophecy is by travelling and hoping we might meet other gods like Ossian who can help us.'

'Or bad ones who might harm us,' muttered Michael.

'Well,' said Clare, 'we'll have to keep a good look out. Get your sacks prepared and let's set out for the loch. I suggest we take it in turns to lead the way. Whoever is in front is to be the scout and has to make a bird call to warn the others of any danger.'

The boys nodded. They were accustomed to that and each could do their own call to perfection.

'Clare,' said Gavin. 'We'd better change our bird calls a little as we're in woodland and not high up on the hill.'

'Good idea,' said Clare. 'I'll be a tawny owl then,' and she put her two hands together and blew through her fingers. A satisfying *hoo-hoo* noise came out.

'Oh, I wanted to be an owl,' said Mot in disappointment. 'She always gets her own way.' He made a face and then said: 'Well, I'll be a magpie.' He made the noisy *kek-kek-kek* cry an alarmed magpie gives. 'What about you, Gavin?'

Gavin thought for a moment: 'I'll make a blackbird's call. I'm not bad at that.' He began trilling the blackbird's call until Clare told him to stop.

'That leaves me,' said Michael with a grin. 'Perhaps I'll just shout "help"!'

'Come on,' said the no-nonsense Clare. 'We've got to get on! Pick your call, Michael.'

So, he made the single *cough-croak* a raven sometimes makes.

'That'll do,' said Clare, 'although it's really a bird of the hills and not the woods. But you'll get away with it. Let's get going!'

They put their spare plaids inside their sacks and put them on. The sacks sat on their backs smoothly and gently and the boys hardly felt any weight. Clare's was heavier and she told the boys that they must switch the iron plate around every hour so that they all took a turn.

'How will we know when an hour is up?' asked Mot. 'We don't have any watches.'

'We'll just have to guess it. Now let's get going.'

Clare stepped out of the cave and round the side of the knoll. Through the birch trees she could see the waters of the loch shining in the sun.

They marched along happily, again feeling nimble and fit, with Mot taking the first turn to be the scout and the rest a little way behind, walking in single file.

The ground was covered in heather and moss, and although the floor of the birch wood was covered in old and broken branches they easily threaded a way through these.

The sun shone and the birches sparkled with the new green leaves of spring. On the big hills they could see the snow had melted, although the highest peaks still had patches of snow on their summits.

They marched on through more woods and over rough moorland. Just when Mot was due to slip back a little for Gavin to take his place as leader, Mot suddenly stopped and silently held up his hand.

The other three immediately halted and crouched down, remaining very still. They all knew that jerky movement in the outdoors attracts inquiring eyes and that animals and birds will often not see a person sitting or standing perfectly still.

Mot made his magpie call and then also crouched down. This was serious stuff.

'Keep very still,' whispered Clare. 'I wonder what's up?'

They could see Mot had wriggled to the top of a little knoll and was peering over it through a thick clump of heather. Clare glanced behind her to see if his head could be seen against the sky, but there was a higher mound behind them.

'Good man, Mot,' she muttered. 'I should have known you would not be caught on the skyline.'

The boys watched intently. Then they saw Mot sliding down.

While still keeping low, he came back to them in a crouching run.

'Clare!' he said. 'It's the oddest thing. The sun is shining, but just ahead of me is a large, flat rock and there's a grey cloud over it like a piece of mist. It's not smoke. There's no fire. It's just hovering over the flat stone.'

Clare listened carefully: 'I think we've had enough of odd stones. Let's all take a squint. Careful now!'

They all moved to the second mound in a crouching run and gathered at its foot.

'No quick movements,' reminded Clare. 'I suggest we all look together rather than having a series of heads bobbing up and down in the one spot.'

They crawled carefully to the top of the mound and slowly parted the heather, gazing through the fronds. There in front of them and on the side of another mound was a large flat stone. The ground fell away steeply to the right and ended in a wide glen or hollow. Just above the stone was a grey cloud. It hovered there and moved backwards and forwards a little, but never really moved from the spot.

'One of us should go forward and see what that's all about,' said Michael.

'Yes,' said Clare. 'I'll go!'

'No you won't,' said Mot. 'I saw it first. Keep down, you lot.'

Before anyone could stop him, he wriggled over the top of the mound and slid down the other side into a little hollow. They watched with keen eyes as he slowly worked his way over to the mound with the stone on it, and then crawled round the back so that the mound and the stone were between him and Clare and the boys.

'Well done, Mot!' said Clare with appreciation. 'He knew better than to approach from the front.'

For a few seconds they could not see anything, just the heather and grass on the mound and the little grey cloud hanging above the flat stone.

Clare didn't really know why, but she felt that something was wrong. 'I don't like this,' she hissed to Michael. 'If you see Mot, signal him to come back.'

They all gazed forward together, but still there was no sign of Mot.

Then they all got a shock. The cloud suddenly moved and then shot out what looked like a long grey arm which landed behind the mound.

There came an anguished shout. It was Mot. He called out once: 'Clare, it's got me!'

And then there was silence.

*The cloud suddenly moved and then shot out what looked like
a long grey arm which landed behind the mound.*

CHAPTER VII

The Dark Men

THE Clan looked on astonished and alarmed as the grey cloud swirled backwards and forwards and then gradually grew black in colour until it looked menacing and evil.

Clare was about to shout that they should all rush forward and see what had happened to Mot, when she saw the cloud changing shape. It became longer and narrower and before their horrified eyes it gradually took on the shape of a person.

'Keep down!' shouted Clare. 'I don't know what's going on, but it hasn't seen us yet. Keep down, no matter what happens.'

The cloud gradually took on the shape of a woman, wearing a dark swirling cloak. Instead of feet she had spread toes, like the talons of a bird. She had long grey hair and her face reminded Clare of the grey and black hooded crow which lived in the hills.

The creature seemed to scan the ground, beady-eyed, looking for weak or ill animals to kill and dead things to eat. She had some kind of bundle under her arm. Clare, for one horrified moment, thought it might be Mot, but saw it was probably part of a dead deer, wrapped in an old piece of cloth.

Gavin picked up a stone. 'I'll let her have it, Clare,' he said.

'No, drop it!' she whispered. 'She doesn't know we're here. Keep an eye out for Mot.'

They all scanned the ground frantically, but could see nothing of him.

Meanwhile, the Being swirled around the knoll, the pointed face and beady eyes looking all around. It seemed only a matter of seconds before she saw the rest of the Clan.

Clare thought hard. 'Let's rush forward,' she said. 'If she's got Mot, then he's bound to be on the other side of the mound. If he *has* escaped and is hiding, we can perhaps drive her away. We'd better make lots of noise and wave our arms. When I say "go!", all dash forward. Get ready.'

Michael and Gavin stood on tip-toe ready to run forward when Clare gave the word to move. But before they could do so, the Being gave a kind of cackle and swooped down before rising up again with Mot clutched under one arm. She seemed to grow bigger and her cloak turned into large, black wings. She looked more fearsome than ever.

She flew over the ground, her long face peering to the right and left.

Clare changed her mind. She desperately wanted to rescue Mot, but she knew that nothing could be done if they were all caught. The Being was now so big, clouding over the sun, that they probably could not frighten it anyway.

So she made a split-second decision. The Being was searching the moor on the far side of the mound and was just turning, getting ready to return to where they were hiding, when Clare saw a little opening in some rocks. There seemed to be room for the three of them, but she wasn't sure how big it was inside.

'Quick! In there!' she said, pointing at the opening. For a second, Michael and Gavin were puzzled because they had been ready to dash forward, but life in the outdoors had prepared them for quick action. They heard Clare's orders, saw her pointing, and quickly dashed into the small cave with Clare fast at their heels. They were just crouching down, when the cave grew dark as the shadow of the Being passed over the entrance.

'What are we to do about Mot?' whispered Gavin. 'We can't just leave him.'

'We're not going to leave him!' snapped Clare. 'But we can't fight a thing that size on our own. It's no good to Mot if we're all caught.'

She crawled to the entrance and looked out. The sun had gone and it seemed very cold. Storm clouds had built up on the mountains. She could see the mound and the flat stone.

'Stay there,' she said to the boys. 'I'm going to take a look.'

She crawled out of the cave and very carefully looked around. She wriggled into some deep heather and gazed down the slope to the wide glen at its foot. Then she saw the Being again.

It had landed like a great grey and black bird at the foot of the glen and she could see what looked like two little buildings. They were hard to pick out because they were the same colour as the trees and moor. For a moment she thought they were boulders. But the more she looked, the more certain she became that they were small dwellings or houses of some kind.

She watched in horror as the Being shrunk again. As she did so, Clare felt the day grow warmer again and the sun started to come out.

The Being pushed the bundle she had under her arm into one of the dwellings and then took another bundle and shoved it into the other house. Then she put a large stone against what seemed to be a door on that building.

Clare thought the second bundle might have been Mot, wrapped up in a plaid so that his arms and legs could not move. She began to feel better. She preferred action. Here was a clear-cut situation. Buildings lay down below. The Being seemed to have put Mot inside one of the buildings. The Clan would go down and get him out.

Having decided on this plan, she crawled back to the cave to give the boys the news.

'I've seen the Creature,' she said to them. 'And I think I saw Mot as well. You see, she flew down to the bottom of the glen. There seem to be some kind of buildings there. I saw her put a bundle in one building and another bundle—which I think was Mot all wrapped up so he couldn't move—into another. What we've got to do now is go down there and get him out.'

41

But the boys didn't seem as excited as she expected.

'Okay, what's up?' asked Clare. 'Didn't you hear what I said? Mot is down there. We've got to get him out. Come on, let's get cracking.'

Michael took hold of her arm. 'Clare,' he said. 'Something strange is going on. There's a light in here.'

'A light? What light?' asked Clare.

Gavin said: 'We were sitting here waiting for you when we realised that the cave went further in. We thought it might turn out to be a better hiding place so we went through that gap there and found ourselves in a bigger cave. Then there was another tunnel. We didn't go any further, but we saw a light.'

'That's right,' said Michael. 'It wasn't daylight getting in through a crack. It flickered, more like a candle.'

'Not only that,' said Gavin. 'We heard voices as well.'

'Voices?' said Clare. 'What do you mean? Are you sure it wasn't the wind or the noise of the burn?'

'No,' said Michael. 'It was like human voices, people talking together.'

'That's right,' agreed Gavin.

'What did you do?' asked Clare.

'Nothing,' said Michael. 'There wasn't time because you were only outside for a few moments. Gavin and I just stayed where we were.'

Gavin nodded.

Clare looked at their serious faces and then said: 'Well we've got to go down and get Mot, but we may need help. Let's go and find your light and see if your voices have bodies attached to them.'

'We'd better be careful,' said Michael. 'They might turn out to be like the Being and not like Ossian.'

'True,' said Gavin. 'We'd better go very carefully *and* quietly.'

'Yes,' said Clare, assuming command again. 'Well, no talking then. Gavin, you lead on—you know where you saw the light.'

They all tip-toed further back into the cave, crawled into a little tunnel and stood upright again in a bigger cave. A little tunnel opened out at one corner. Gavin stopped and pointed. Clare looked in. Further along the corridor was a little flame, flickering and sending out quite a lot of light, throwing their shadows on to the walls.

They paused and Michael and Gavin looked inquiringly at Clare.

'Should we go on?' whispered Michael.

'Yes,' said Clare, and tip-toed towards the flickering flame.

When Clare, Michael and Gavin had reached the flame they stopped for a few seconds. It seemed to be some kind of oil lamp. The oil lay in a little, hollowed out stone with a long rush coming out of it. The rush burned like the wick of a candle. It didn't smell very nice and it didn't look as if it would burn for long.

'It smells like fish,' said Gavin, wrinkling up his nose. Clare nodded in agreement. It did smell of fish.

She signalled for them to move on and then they saw a second light where the tunnel appeared to take another bend. Again they moved forward silently and with great care. The deer skin currans on their feet were both quiet and comfortable.

When they came round a corner, they all suddenly leapt in fright as a small figure rose up in front of them, saying: 'Halt!'

He had been sitting on a stone at the side of the tunnel. Clare thought he had perhaps fallen asleep and had only awakened when they were almost on top of him.

'Who are you?' she gasped, trying to examine him in the poor light. She saw he was holding a short spear and kept pointing it at her, so she held up her hand to show that she was not carrying any weapon. She was beginning to understand the reason for this open-hand salute that they were all getting so accustomed to.

'I am Tormud, son of Cormac. I and my friend Eoghann guard this entry against all enemies and strangers. Who are you, girl? Come forward and let me see you in the light.'

Clare came forward and her green dress and gold head-band shone in the flickering flame. Tormud gave a kind of bow. 'Forgive me, oh Princess,' he said. 'I did not know you were of the royal house.'

Clare replied with confidence: 'Tormud'—she was getting the hang of the strange speech—'I and my brothers and my friend were journeying towards our own land when we saw a strange cloud. It turned into a kind of witch and took my brother away. We were hiding in your cave when we saw your light.'

Tormud waved his spear: 'You have seen the Cailleach Bheur, the Witch-of-the-Storms. She is very evil. She has a magic house not far from here, but she has been far away visiting her sister who is also evil. The Cailleach Bheur creates storms on the seas and drowns many sailors. Did you not feel the air grow cold and the storms gather when you saw the creature?'

Clare nodded: 'Yes indeed, Tormud. I saw the weather change and wondered why. When she flew away the sun came out again. She holds my brother, Mot, as a prisoner. What can we do? Can you help us?'

Tormud gazed past Clare to where Michael and Gavin stood silently. He asked: 'Are you the attendants and guards of this princess?'

Clare replied: 'This is my brother, Michael, and my friend, Gavin. We met Ossian, son of Fionn, and he helped us. We have a magic prophecy which we must fulfill before we can return to our own land.'

Tormud thought for a moment: 'We must rescue your brother, but we will need help. My friend Eoghann will be back soon and he can guard the cave. I was about to return and he will not be alarmed. Follow me and I will take you to my people. Together we can plan to outwit the witch and rescue your brother.

'It is good that she is in her house in the glen, because she has other homes on top of high mountains. It would be much harder to defeat her there. Can you all walk long distances?'

'Yes,' said Michael. 'We have had a good breakfast. Ossian gave us barley cakes and honey and we also have dramach with us in our pouches.'

'We're fit as well,' added Gavin. 'We can walk a long way without getting tired.'

Tormud nodded in approval. 'You will have to travel a long way to find my friends. I and Eoghann were sent to guard this tunnel, but now that the Cailleach Bheur is in her house she will stay there for a long time. But we always have one guard, in case she goes hunting sooner than we think.

'These houses which she took by magic once belonged to my people. Gather round and I will tell you about them.'

Clare, Michael and Gavin sat down at his feet. In the flickering light Tormud told them how his people had lived at the lochsides and in the glens and straths. When spring came they had taken their cattle and goats and headed for the upper glens and the high moors and the fresh grass.

There they had seen their animals grow fat and healthy and they made cheese and butter from their milk. They had built temporary houses, called shielings, of stone walls and a turf roof. There they stayed until the end of summer when they went back down to the lower ground again.

'These were lovely days,' said Tormud with a smile. 'We sang songs and made poems. People married one another there. We had happy days when we ran races and tried to throw stones further than our friends could. We even had spear contests,' he added. 'We would take a heavy war-spear and put both hands beneath one end and then hurl it up into the air so that it would fall out of the sky on enemies like the Cailleach Bheur.'

Then he murmured sadly: 'But her magic is strong and she can now turn our spears back on us.'

Clare thought for a moment: 'You know, in our country we have games as well, called Highland Games, and we run races and hurl stones and heave a tree-trunk called a caber into the air so that it falls in a straight line. It shows how strong some people are.'

Tormud smiled again: 'That sounds like our happy days at the shielings. You are from a different time and race, but perhaps these things you do are not all that different after all.'

Michael said: 'Clare, you did not tell Tormud about the prophecy? Perhaps he could help us with it?'

Clare nodded: 'Tormud, at the time we were carried off from our own land, we had just been looking at a grey boulder through three holes in a deer antler.

'Well, a storm rose and we lost our senses for a time. When we awoke we were dressed like this. We had found a piece of wood in an old chest and it had words carved on it. Ossian told us that we had to fulfill all the things in the prophecy before we could return to our own land.'

Tormud nodded gravely and said: 'Say it for me, oh Princess.'

Gavin handed his notebook to Clare who recited the poem slowly and steadily. When she had finished there was silence for a moment, and then she said: 'We have completed one task. We met Ossian, who is a harper and a bard. But we do not know where to go next.'

Tormud looked very excited. 'My people have a special horn,' he said. 'But none of us can blow it. There is an old tale that if it is blown, then the warriors from the past—the Fianne, who are called after the great god Fionn—will rise up and come to the aid of people in their hour of need.

'The horn is very old and covered in jewels and we keep it on the wall of one of our caves, but we cannot get any sound from it. Come and I will show it to you and you can meet my friends and our father and leader, Cormac. Perhaps they can help you to get your brother, Mot, returned safely to you. But first we have to go out of the cave again for a time and then we go back into the ground once more. Follow me!'

He turned and moved off into the darkness. Without hesitation he kept going through what seemed to be an endless cave. Clare, Michael and Gavin followed him, bumping into the walls because they were not so accustomed to the dark. Every now and again they seemed to pass other openings which led off to the sides. When that happened Tormud waited until they had all closed up together so that no one was lost. Then they moved off again.

The tunnel grew lighter and they emerged on to the open hillside. Tormud made them go back inside the entrance while he scouted around and then he came back and said all was well. He made them sit down in the entrance until their eyes grew more accustomed to the light.

Once they were outside Tormud and the children looked at one another more closely. He seemed quite an old man, but was very short in height (about the height of Mot, Gavin thought). He had black hair cut in a straight line over his forehead and wore a long shirt of a kind of yellow-brown colour which Clare later discovered was called saffron. It seemed to her to be made of linen. He also had a long deer skin jacket which went down over his hips. Below his long shirt he wore long, slim, deer skin boots which came up almost to his knees. They were like wellington boots, Clare thought, but not fat and flappy. They fitted closely to his legs. He carried a little bag on his back similar to their own and his spear had a very sharp, broad blade on it.

Tormud's face was pale, like someone who has been ill or who spends a lot of time in the dark. When he smiled his teeth were very white.

He saw the children examining him and looked kindly at them. 'Have you never seen one of my race before?' he asked.

'Never,' said Clare. Then she noticed that his arms and knees were covered in a kind of tattoo: intricate whorled lines, linked and seemingly endless snakes running into one another, similar to the design of the brooches they wore. They seemed to have been painted on, like war-paint, and were mainly blue in colour.

Tormud saw her looking at his arms and smiled: 'We are the

people who possessed the land before history, but we are not big men and enemies defeated us. We now live in caves in the rocks.'

He stopped and his eyes went blank as if asleep. Then he said in a sing-song voice, like someone in a trance: 'In later times strange men are to come to this land. They will have red cloaks, and swords and horses, and their armies will move in great bands of men called legions. So the seers and prophets say.'

'It sounds like the Romans,' muttered Michael, looking at Clare for agreement.

She nodded and signalled to the boys to stay quiet while Tormud was in a trance. He continued in his sing-song voice: 'They will call us the Picts, the painted people. The land was ours before the other races came. Some of us will marry them. Some of us will fight them. Our kings might have sons who will have sons who will become their kings. But I will not see it.'

He gave a kind of start and his eyes opened. He stayed silent for a moment and then said sadly: 'We are the small dark men. There are not many of us left. Come, I will take you to my father.'

'Where are we going?' asked Gavin.

'Do you see that loch?' Tormud said, pointing off into the distance.

'Yes,' chorused Michael and Gavin.

'It is called Loch Katrine—the loch of the bristly or rough places,' said Tormud. 'Close by is a mountain called Beinn Venue, which means it has many caves. There my people live in the Corrie-of-the-Goblins. Do you know what a corrie is?' he asked.

'A big hollow in the hills,' said Clare. 'Or a cauldron—but it will be a hollow here, surely.'

'You are right,' said Tormud.

'Are there really goblins?' asked Michael.

Tormud smiled again. 'Yes. They no longer live in their caves, but in the air and in the trees. They are happier there. *We* now live in their caves, the small dark men. Come now, I will show you.'

He set off across the heather at a brisk pace and they saw again that their new friend was smaller than they were.

Clare, Michael and Gavin followed him, their minds still on Mot and his fate. Clare was upset. She didn't want to leave the area where they had last seen Mot, but she knew help was needed.

Her eyes rested on Michael and Gavin marching along and she admired their strong tanned legs and the way they were striding out, fearlessly. She also thought what a good garment for the outdoors their plaid kilts were.

The sun occasionally glinted on Tormud's spear and that cheered her up as well. Surely he would protect them until they reached the Corrie-of-the-Goblins.

She took courage from that and, raising her chin in the brave and dignified way she felt a leader and a princess should, she marched on into the hills.

CHAPTER VIII

The Magic Horn

THEIR route took them over rough moorland. Occasionally Tormud would stop beside boulders and take them underground for a time and they would stumble through a series of caves in which he was totally at home. Just when they were getting used to it, he would suddenly emerge into the open air again.

But the loch he called Katrine grew nearer and nearer and soon he was picking his way round the side of the mountain and above the water of the loch. The ground grew rougher and the grass and heather changed to stony ground and layers of small broken-up stones called scree.

Tormud began to clamber uphill where there was a huge mass of jumbled boulders, honeycombed with holes and caves. Just when it seemed he was going to go underground again, he suddenly stood on top of a large boulder and let out the kind of bellow a stag makes in the autumn when they are fighting one another to keep as many hinds as possible.

Clare, Michael and Gavin stood still as Tormud's bellow echoed among the rocks. Suddenly another man appeared on top of a large stone. He too had a spear and he looked at them closely before signalling Tormud to come forward.

Tormud spoke to him and occasionally turned round and pointed to the children and then turned back to talk again. Then he waved them forward.

'We are going underground into a huge cave,' he said to Clare. 'You must all promise that you will never reveal its where-abouts.'

'I promise,' said Clare.

'So do I,' chorused Gavin and Michael.

'Come then,' said Tormud. 'Follow me!' He began clambering uphill again over more boulders. Then he went alongside a little burn which trickled down between the rocks until he came to a kind of grassy bowl or large hollow in the rocks which was surprisingly big and which could not be seen from below.

'This is the Corrie-of-the-Goblins,' he said. 'There is room for over thirty men to meet here and not be seen from the glen below.' Then he turned and entered a narrow passage which the children had not seen.

They were growing accustomed to diving in and out of the darkness so they followed him without hesitation.

The caves and tunnels were lit by the little oil lamps they had seen before. Tormud told them that the oil came from seals and was brought far inland in waterproof jars. Every now and again the dim lights were replaced by a bright flaring light, like a taper. Tormud said these were made from pine cones. Beside the bright lights, but hidden in a shadowy alcove, was a sentry with a spear who stepped out and challenged them. When he saw Tormud, he went back into the shadows and sat down on a little stone seat.

'Someone reported that the Cailleach Bheur was flying and hunting today,' said Tormud. 'Everyone is being careful, but we should be safe here. There are too many of us in this place for her to defeat us all.'

Then the children got a shock.

For Tormud suddenly emerged into a huge cavern or cave and it seemed to be thronged with people. A little underground burn ran through one side of the cave and the roof seemed so high that it was lost in the darkness.

Along another wall were little sleeping shelters, like cubicles, made of wooden frames and deer skin hangings with heather beds inside. In the middle of the cave burned a huge fire. The smoke must have found a way out through the rocks because it did not swirl around the cave but went up into the darkness.

'Cracked gaps in the rocks break the smoke up and by the time it reaches the surface it is hard to see against the stones on the outside,' explained Tormud.

At one side of the fire men and women were looking after large cauldrons which seemed to contain some kind of stew. The smell was delicious.

At the back of the cave was a kind of stone throne partly covered in deer skins. On it sat a very old man, with a very long beard, wearing crimson robes. He had a silver crown on his forehead with a twisted band on it which looked like a snake. In his hand he held a white staff.

Tormud led the way towards him, saying: 'Oh father, these are the children the messengers have told you about. This is the Princess Clare and her brother and her friend, Michael and Gavin, who are her guards and attendants.

'As you have been told, another brother, Mot, has been taken by the Cailleach Bheur. They need your help.'

The old man looked at them as if he could not hear properly and then he gave a grave smile. Pointing at Clare with the white staff he said: 'Oh Princess, you are welcome to the Corrie-of-the-Goblins, the last refuge of my people. Rest and eat and we will talk again soon.'

He closed his eyes and seemed to doze.

Tormud signalled to them that the interview was over and took them to the fire where men and women, all looking very alike with their deer skin tunics, black hair and small stature, served them food—hot, deer meat stew in wooden bowls, barley bread scones and flagons of milk. Clare examined her flagon, and realised it had been carved from the horn of a cow or bull.

'Sleep now,' said Tormud, 'and then I will ask my father to let you see the sacred horn I told you of. Then we will plan how to rescue your brother.'

Clare began to protest that she didn't want to sleep. There was no time to waste, she insisted. They had to get going to rescue Mot. She began to tell Tormud that she needed all his friends with their spears ... when she fell asleep ... in mid sentence.

When Clare woke up she felt refreshed. Had some kind of mild sleeping potion been put in their food, she wondered?

Gavin and Michael were also awake and were just putting their spare plaids back into their sacks and were on the point of demanding action when Tormud appeared and said, 'Follow me.'

He took them out of the busy cavern into a side tunnel and they emerged into another cave. Tormud's father stood beside one wall, leaning on his white staff and still wearing his crown with the snake crest.

The old man turned to Clare and said: 'I wear a crown with a snake emblem, the endless twisting line that is both life and death and which you have carved on your brooch. I have the white staff which is a special colour and which means peace and wise rule. Both of these things have been held by my race for many years. But I may be the last of my line as we get fewer in number each year.

'We do not know where the sacred horn came from. We only know that our people owned it in the dim years which had no beginning and that we cannot get it to make any sound.

'Our seers and storytellers say that if it is blown then the Fianne, the warriors of Fionn, will appear and come to our aid.'

He turned his gaze to Clare and continued: 'My child, my son Tormud tells me you have a prophecy which will help you get back to your own time and your own people once you have fulfilled every aspect, and that you have been asked to find a magic horn.

'Perhaps you might have the answer to our secret as well. Ask your brother and his friend to arise. This must be done in a fitting fashion.'

Michael and Gavin stood up and the old king gave each a white staff to hold. With a little jar of blue paint he marked snake-like whorls on their arms and legs. Then he did the same to Tormud.

'Now we are ready,' he said. 'We have the staff of peace and wise rule and the snakes of life and death. Blow, child! Our fate lies with you.'

Clare stood very straight in her green dress, her gold headband flashing in the light of the flaring torches and lamps. She took from the king an old horn, made of the horn of some giant cow or bull long ago and now covered in precious stones, pearls, amethysts, garnets and other crystals which had been found in the rocks and the rivers and burns.

She made a little face and wet her lips with her tongue. She put the horn to her lips, sucked in her breath and then blew hard.

A great, blaring noise came from the horn. It rattled around the walls of the cavern and they could hear it echoing along miles of caves and tunnels, getting fainter and fainter as it went further away from them. Their heads reeled with the noise. They could hear alarmed shouts from the other caves as the small men and women heard a sacred noise they had never heard before and would never hear again.

Clare took the horn from her lips, paused, and blew a second blast. Then all the flares and torches in the cave went out.

All was black.

Clare put the horn to her lips, sucked in her breath and then blew hard.

CHAPTER IX

The Fianne at War

CLARE, Michael and Gavin stood blinking in bright sunshine, looking around in astonishment. They were no longer in the cave. They were outside on the open hillside and seemed to be a long way from the Corrie-of-the-Goblins. There was no sign of the small dark men and women.

'What on earth happened?' asked Michael, shading his eyes from the sun.

'Some kind of spell,' murmured Clare in amazement. 'I blew the horn and the next thing I knew we're out here in the open. Where have Tormud's people gone?'

The children stood staring at the boulders in the Corrie, but could see no sign of life.

'We'd better go back and take a look,' said Clare.

'What a nuisance,' muttered Gavin. 'Why have we been dumped here only to walk back again?'

'I don't know,' sighed Michael. 'But we can't go from here without trying to find out.'

'You two—save your breath for the climb up,' said Clare as they toiled back up over the steepening slopes of heather and grass. Eventually they reached the boulders and clambered up on to them.

'Don't make too much noise,' whispered Clare. 'Remember, we're not far from the Cailleach Bheur's house.'

Gavin looked peeved: 'How can *we* make too much noise? What about that trumpet blast of yours? It could be heard miles away.'

'Shhhh,' hushed Clare. She looked around herself, mystified. 'You know, I don't see any of the holes or caves we were in before. Scout around, you two—see if you can see anything or anybody.'

Michael and Gavin clambered all over the rocks, but could see no opening which was familiar to them. They reported to Clare that even the large, open, grassy section which Tormud had pointed out to them seemed to have gone.

'Let's take part of the rocks each,' said Clare, 'and try calling down into the caves. Not too loudly.'

So they clambered and wandered around and went into some caves and then came out again and reported to Clare that they could find no tunnels. They called down into holes, but got no reply other than a scrabbling noise in one of the caves which might have been a fox.

Of the old king and Tormud and their small friends there was no sign. In fact, they were never to see them again, but they did not know that at the time.

'What'll we do now, Clare?' asked Gavin.

'Well, we've still got our sacks and our plaids and things,' said Clare. 'We should continue to walk around the shores of the loch in the hope of meeting someone. That's the best plan for the moment anyhow. But only for a short while. We can't leave Mot much longer.'

They had hardly reached the shore of the loch when Gavin saw a large prominent rock on a mound, like a kind of tower, he thought, and he pointed it out to Clare and Michael.

'We can see a long way from there,' he said. 'If we don't find anyone else to help, then we must go back and try to rescue Mot on our own.'

'I was thinking the same thing,' said Clare. 'This is our last chance to find help. After that, we can't wait any longer.'

They reached the mound and clambered up on top of the rock. It had a kind of twisting section on one side rather like big stone steps.

'Clare,' said Michael. 'Look at these. Someone has made them.'
Gavin and Clare examined the steps.

'So they have,' she said. 'How odd! Well, let's get to the top and have a look.'

She reached the top of the rock tower and they found there was room for the three of them to gather on top. A piece of rock made a natural seat and Clare sat down on it. The boys sat at her feet on either side, gazing over the silver waters of the lochs and what seemed to be endless birch woods.

Clare felt hot after her clamber up and she took off her plaid and put it on the rock seat and sat on it, feeling the cool wind gently touching her green dress. She took off her gold headband, wiped it on a corner of the plaid and put it back on.

Then she fell silent, but she wasn't asleep. She was doing her utmost to think of a plan to rescue Mot. Suddenly she had a brainwave. She smacked her knee with her hand and muttered, 'I've got it! The feathers! The ptarmigan feathers ... the ones Ossian gave us! What a fool I've been! Why didn't I think of it before? They are supposed to act like a charm, to ward off evil. I bet they'll frighten the Cailleach Bheur. It's worth a try.'

She delved into her sack and pulled out the little cluster of white and black feathers and examined them. They looked very white in the bright sunlight. She remembered that old King Cormac and Tormud had both said that white was a special colour long ago and they had white staffs for that reason.

She took a feather from each end of the cluster and gave one to Gavin and one to Michael: 'Hang on to these. We should each have something to protect us in case we get split up.'

Clare tapped her chest three times with the feathers as Ossian had said, waved the rest of the feathers triumphantly, saying: 'Great! We'll show *her*. Let's just march over there and get Mot out.'

The boys gave a kind of cheer and scrambled to their feet. Gavin started to say that they should really stay hidden until the last minute, but instead he gave a kind of gasp and broke off in mid sentence.

'What's the matter with you?' asked Clare, glaring at him.

'Look!' said Gavin, pointing towards the loch. 'Someone's coming.'

'So there is,' said Clare, looking across the heather to where a tall man was walking towards them.

He seemed to be wearing some kind of armour on his chest and a helmet which glinted in the sun. He had long fair hair and a big, drooping moustache. He carried a shield and an axe and his clothes were of saffron brown like the small dark men, but he was nearly twice as tall.

He was barefoot, but his feet and legs were dark brown from the sun and his legs and feet looked tough and sinewy.

'Hey, there's another!' gasped Gavin, pointing in the opposite direction. Sure enough, another man was walking towards them, this time carrying a spear.

'There's more!' shouted Michael, waving his hand towards the loch where a little band of men, all armed and dressed like the other in brown clothes, walked or ran across the heather towards the children. They all waved their weapons and shouted. For a moment, Clare was rooted to the spot.

'Should we run for it?' asked Gavin.

'No, it's too late,' said Clare. 'Look!'

From the lochside came more men, this time on horseback, riding without saddles. Then came others, standing upright in little, single, two wheeled chariots pulled by one horse. The chariots bumped and swayed over the heather.

They moved towards the children until they were surrounded by dozens of armed men who formed a ring around the rock and stared up at them. More and more came from the lochside and from the nearby glen: some with bows and arrows, some with swords and axes, all with shining helmets and armour on their chests.

A silence fell and the children looked uneasily at them and at one another.

Then Clare had a brainwave. She stepped forward, a slim figure in her green dress and gold headband and held up her hand with her bare palm showing.

To her astonishment, all the men knelt down on one knee in front of her.

CHAPTER X

The Magic Spring

CLARE looked down on the kneeling men and wondered what to do next. Then a man stepped forward and stared at her. He had a gold band around his neck, like Clare's headband, but with a gap in the ring at the front. At each end there was a carved snake's head. Clare later learned such rings were called *torcs*.

He bowed to Clare and she was about to curtsey when she felt that if she inclined her head a little that would do. She was beginning to get the hang of being royalty.

The man then spoke to her: 'Oh, Queen,' he said, 'we are the Fianne, the warriors of the great god Fionn. From over the years and from many lands we have heard the magic horn blow and we have now arisen from our graves to do whatever service you command.

'All we ask, Queen, is that your task for us last only until the setting sun, because it is then that we must return to the lands of our ancestors and to the days when we ruled these hills and glens.'

Clare, secretly very pleased at being called Queen, listened to this gravely and then said: 'I hear you, oh warrior of the great Fianne. What is your name?'

'I am called Conn,' the man said. 'What is your bidding?'

Clare said: 'Tell your men to sit down and rest and I will tell you of our adventures and of our hour of need.'

Conn gave a little smile and said: 'We will sit because you have commanded it, but we never tire.'

The men of the Fianne sat down in the heather, placing their weapons beside them. They began to talk quietly to one another while Clare descended the rock tower, accompanied by the unusually silent Gavin and Michael.

Finding his voice, Michael poked Clare in the back and whispered, 'You've been promoted, oh Princess. Now you're a Queen. So what does that make us?'

'The court jesters,' retorted Clare. 'Now shut up, and do what you're told.'

Conn met her at the foot of the rock and led her to a piece of smooth grass and then put a kind of cloak on the ground for her to sit on. 'Now, tell me everything,' he said.

Clare told her story—the moving boulder, the antler with the three holes, the carved piece of wood, the prophecy, their meeting with Ossian, the Cailleach Bheur and the small, dark people. His eyes grew grave when she mentioned the prophecy and he nodded in approval when she said they had fulfilled two of the tasks—meeting Ossian, the bard, and blowing the magic horn.

She told of how the Cailleach Bheur had snatched Mot and Conn's face grew cold with anger. She said she had ptarmigan feathers, but had forgotten these until a few minutes before the Fianne arrived.

Conn leapt up. 'You have ptarmigan feathers? The feathers of the mother bird of all? We will be victorious! We will defeat the Cailleach Bheur. She cannot stand against a charm of that kind. I will tell the warriors.'

He turned and shouted to them that Clare had a special talisman—the white feathers of the ptarmigan. The men cheered and began to talk to one another in excited tones, sounding like a swarm of bees.

Conn went on: 'Oh Queen, I can help you with two of the prophecies. You must travel to the far off lands of the west. There in a glen and beside a loch called Etive—the name of a storm goddess—you will meet another princess. She is called Deirdre and is noted for her beauty. Find her bower or home. She will help you because she has had much sadness in her life. She is the "maid forlorn" mentioned in your prophecy.'

He picked up his spear and said to Clare: 'I now know how to defeat your witch and to give you the secret of another of your tasks. Did the Cailleach Bheur stop beside a flat stone on the hillside and hover above it in the shape of a cloud?'

'Yes, she did,' said Clare, excited at the thought of action.

Conn continued: 'A magic spring lies beneath that stone. Each day she takes the stone away and water with magic power flows out so that she can drink of it. She puts the stone back each night otherwise the water would run for ever and flood the glen below and her house as well.

'There are other magic springs like that. If you were to travel northwards to a loch called Tay, you would find it was born of a magic spring that ran forever. And when you are in the west seeking Deirdre you will find another loch born of the same waters—it is called Awe.

'Come, I will show you how to get rid of that witch, now that we have the magic feathers, and we will rescue your brother.'

He took the ptarmigan feathers from Clare and tied nearly all of them to the head of his spear. Then he gave a few to another warrior. When he held his spear up, all the men cheered.

He signalled for a number of men to come forward, men of rank, with torcs round their necks like his own, but this time of silver. He gave them orders and they went back to the other warriors and spoke at length to them.

'Stand beside me, Queen, at all times,' said Conn. 'Ask your brother and friend to do the same.'

Clare turned to the boys and said: 'Stick by me! Okay?'

'Yes, oh Queen,' said Gavin with a grin. Michael giggled. Clare shot them a withering look and turned back to Conn.

He faced the warriors and raised his spear. They all rose to their feet.

'Men of the Fianne!' he shouted. 'Let us go to war!'

CHAPTER XI

The Golden Wall

CONN led a long procession of men across the hillside. Clare, Gavin and Michael did not have to walk, however. Warriors came forward with shields to which they had attached long poles. They helped the children to sit on them and then they carried them across the heather and grass at great speed.

'Forward!' shouted Conn, holding up his spear with the ptarmigan feathers. Each time he did so the men roared a war-cry.

Soon they reached the mound and the flat stone where the children had seen the Cailleach Bheur. The warriors of the Fianne spread out in a ring around the bottom of the mound.

Conn ordered his men to carry Clare, Michael and Gavin over to the stone and he examined it carefully.

He tried to lift it by himself, but it was too heavy. He signalled for more men to help. Clare, Michael and Gavin also held the sides, trying to move it.

The men pushed and grunted. With a loud scraping noise the stone moved sideways and a little, clear rivulet of water bubbled out and began to run down the hillside.

Just then there was a loud screaming noise from below and a black cloud began to form, taking on the shape of a woman. She flew towards them, her beak long and threatening, her eyes ablaze with anger, talons bared and wings spread out like those of a giant bird.

She hovered around for a moment and then headed straight for them, screaming all the time. Clare, Michael and Gavin crouched down and the Fianne began to hurl spears and shoot arrows at her, but she brushed them off and still came on at them.

Conn leapt forward and held up his spear with the ptarmigan feathers attached to it and the Cailleach Bheur halted in mid air and hovered there again, screeching all the time and flapping her wings.

The warriors hurled more spears and arrows at her and the Cailleach Bheur began to fly around in circles, still screeching angrily.

Clare was so busy watching her that she did not notice that the little spring at their feet was now gushing out in great waves of water, like a waterfall in flood or a tap which has been turned on full.

It began to foam down the hillside. As they all watched, it grew bigger and wider until soon it was like a river in flood, carrying bits of heather and grass and stones with it, which began to roll down hill under the force of the water.

The Cailleach Bheur screeched again out of the skies: 'Stop it! Stop it! You are releasing the magic spring! Stop it! Stop it!'

Conn laughed. 'It cannot be stopped now,' he shouted.

Clare, Gavin and Michael looked on in amazement as the burn roared and widened and the bottom of the glen began to fill up with water and to spread out and form the start of a new loch.

The Cailleach Bheur flew low overhead, cackling with rage, but something strange had happened to her. She seemed to be getting smaller, Clare thought—less frightening.

She flew lower and lower and her cackles grew less fierce. Then one of the Fianne's arrows struck her and she flopped down even lower and splashed into the by now roaring river and was carried downhill.

Soon there was nothing to be seen or heard but the rumble of the water and the splash of new waterfalls. The children heaved sighs of relief.

'I think that she is gone for ever,' said Conn.

But Clare did not rejoice for long. She gazed at the flooded glen and the roaring torrent and saw that the new loch was widening and growing by the second.

Soon it was lapping around the buildings where the Cailleach Bheur had imprisoned Mot.

She grabbed Conn's arm. 'My brother is down there! He was put inside that building by the witch. Soon it will be under water. We've got to do something—quickly!'

Conn's face was calm. 'Do not worry, Queen,' he said. 'When I gave my orders for the Fianne to attack I sent men to both houses. One contained her book of spells and special objects she uses for magic, and where she keeps food. We have left these to be drowned and cleansed in the clear waters of the magic spring.

'The other held your brother. They will have rescued him by now. Then they will bring him to you. See, they come now.'

Clare gazed down the hillside and Gavin and Michael let out a little cheer as a small group of men came uphill carrying a shield on long poles. On it sat Mot, looking as cheery as ever.

When they grew near, Mot gave a wave and said: 'Hello, you lot! I'm not kidding, but that really shook me up. I got the fright of my life when she grabbed me.

'She put a kind of spell on me and I couldn't move. Then she stuck me in that building and I couldn't get the door open. She put some kind of heavy boulder outside. I tried to get through the roof but she had put stones on top of the turf and I couldn't find an opening. *What* an adventure! Imagine flying and nearly being drowned all at the same time.'

Clare nearly cried with relief at seeing Mot again and Michael and Gavin went across and clapped him on the shoulder.

Mot, embarrassed, shrugged them off. 'Calm down, calm down!' he said. 'There's no need to fuss. I thought you would mount a rescue bid, but I was getting a little bit alarmed when nothing happened for over a day. It seemed an eternity.'

He looked at the men of the Fianne who were now sitting on the hillside watching the loch grow bigger and bigger.

'I must say I'm impressed,' he said. 'Where did you meet all these men?'

Clare told him of meeting the small, dark men and blowing the horn and how Conn and the Fianne had come to their rescue.

'Yes, but that's not all,' said Gavin. 'We've completed another section of the prophecy and our tasks—the magic horn and now the magic spring.'

'Yes,' said Michael. 'And Conn says now we have to travel to the west to meet a princess called Deirdre and she will help us.'

Mot digested all this news while the Fianne began to gather into bands and groups again.

Conn went up to Clare and bowed and said: 'The day passes, Queen. We must return to The Land Beyond The Sunset as it is ordained.'

Clare began to thank him, but he halted her, saying: 'You blew the magic horn. In the years ahead some other person will find this horn in a cave and they should blow it also. We will arise again and come to the aid of the land of Scotland and its people. Let us say farewell to you now.'

Clare, Gavin, Michael and Mot stood together in a little group as the Fianne were drawn up in ranks in front of them—tall, fierce men with their armour, their helmets, axes, spears and bows shining in the evening sun.

Conn gave an order and they all saluted Clare by raising their weapons in their right hands and then kneeling on one knee. She held her hand up, palm forward, and gave a kind of salute, moving from one end of the line to the other. The boys also stood up and raised their hands.

They were all silent as the men marched away and then the evening light dimmed and there was no sound to be heard, but the ripple of the ever-running burn and the widening loch and the call of the blackbirds and thrushes in the trees and the larks singing on the moors.

Their eyes followed the warriors over the moorland and through the woods until they could no longer be sure they were seeing their brown clothes or just bracken; or whether the grey horses pulling the chariots were really just far-off boulders and the sunlight on their weapons only glinting water.

* * *

By now the children were tired out by their adventure and flopped down on the grass.

The evening sun sank beneath the horizon, picking out the far off mountains in blue and purple. The sky grew golden in the west, with flecks of red light.

Clare looked at it with pleasure. 'That's where we're going tomorrow,' she said. 'To the west, to meet the Princess Deirdre. Perhaps we might get home after all.'

The setting sun caught the remaining flecks of cloud and tinged them with gold. The far-off sky shone with a glowing yellow colour.

Gavin tugged excitedly at Clare's arm. 'Clare!' he said. 'That's where we're going, to "the golden wall of the west". Well, there's the golden wall—the land of the setting sun. So, we've found another part of the prophecy and of our tasks.'

Clare stared at the sky. 'I think you're right,' she said thoughtfully. Michael and Mot nodded agreement and they all gazed with growing excitement at the late evening sky as the yellow light shone and then began to fade.

'Let's sleep now,' said Clare. 'We have a long way to go when the new day starts.'

CHAPTER XII

The Journey

THEN came the longest part of the Clan's journey. They seemed to travel for many days to get to the west and they slept in caves, on the hillsides and in the woods.

Gavin remembered reading about a way of sleeping out of doors, so when they could not find a cave they followed his instructions. They cut a large 'bed' of heather and then cut other bundles which they laid alongside.

They then took it in turns to be the last person 'in', and three of them would lie down on the bed of heather and leave a gap in the middle for the fourth. The person left outside would then ensure they were all well tucked into their extra belted plaids and then place the bundles of heather over them to form a kind of roof, leaving a gap for the last person.

Once they were all settled, the last person would slip into the gap and pull a bundle of heather down into the remaining hole in the 'roof' and they would all sleep well.

They all knew that cold and damp come through the ground at night and that in the night or early morning dew will soak everything, but they all seemed to be tougher and able to stand the cold and wet better than in their own world.

Gavin's idea for bedding worked well and he almost blushed with pleasure when the rest of the Clan praised his brainwave. Before they moved on the next day they would carry the heather some way off and then scatter it around so they left little trace of their presence.

Clare began to worry that they would run short of food and one day they had to eat some of their dramach. It tasted horrible, like cold porridge, but it did give them energy.

Strangely they found as they journeyed that sometimes food was left beside the path. This puzzled them until Clare saw some people watching them through the trees. She called to them and waved, but they vanished and she had no idea who they were.

They felt quite often that they were being watched, but no one harmed them and they thought it might be because they had attached ptarmigan feathers to their bonnets.

They held a conference about this one day.

'Who's doing it?' asked Clare. 'Who's leaving the food? Why are they doing it?'

'They are very good at hiding,' said Mot. 'We keep trying to spot them, but they just vanish. Perhaps they are hunters from another land and good at travelling fast and staying hidden.'

'Yes,' agreed Michael. 'But have you noticed something else? They always leave the food on green, grassy mounds, little hills shaped like cones. Why are they doing that?'

Gavin chipped in excitedly: 'Hey! I think I know about that. I remember Aunt Elspeth telling me. She said that hills shaped like cones were believed to be places where faeries lived in past times. She said that if you saw the name "sithich" on a map it often meant a faery hill. The faeries were called the People of Quietness,' he added.

Clare nodded, but she was about to heap scorn on the idea when she remembered that they had experienced quite a lot of magic in the past few days and tales of faeries might well be true in this land and time where they had been stranded.

'Yes, but that's not all,' said Gavin, his voice rising a little with his new found wisdom. 'These people believed the cuckoo did not migrate overseas at the end of summer, but stayed inside these hills and came out again in the spring.'

Mot gasped: 'The cuckoo! That's another of our prophecies and tasks. If we keep passing these faery mounds and hills, then we should keep our ears and eyes open in case we hear or see a cuckoo. After all, we're into the spring now.'

Clare thought for a moment. 'Well ... ,' she said slowly, 'I suppose that would explain a lot. It would explain why the food is always fresh and why it's lying beside the path just when we come along. These beings or people must be able to see us, but we can't always see them.

'After all, if the food was left for any length of time, it would go rotten, or the crows or ravens would eat it, or a fox would take it.'

'Perhaps wolves would as well,' said Gavin. 'If there *are* wolves here?' he added. 'After all, we're back in time.'

Clare, Michael and Mot looked slightly perturbed. 'Wolves!' said Clare. 'I hadn't thought of that.'

'I don't think they attack people though,' said Gavin. 'I read that somewhere. They just move around in packs and attack other animals.'

'Well, that's a relief,' said Clare. 'But we've still got to be careful. After all, the prophecy speaks of dogs that can kill. We don't know what that means. We'd better make sure that our ptarmigan feathers are all safe. I suggest that only I keep one or two on my bonnet to protect us all. The rest can go into our sporrans.'

'Good idea,' said Michael, so they all did that.

'I've been thinking about all this,' said Clare. 'I think these people who are watching us, who we hardly ever see, think we're some kind of magic being like themselves. That would explain why they always leave the food on these faery mounds.

'They *must* watch us, work out where we're likely to go and then dash ahead. They seem to leave enough food for each day.'

Gavin nodded with relish. It was one of the pleasures of their journey that each evening they would halt and Clare would build a little fire in a place where it could not easily be seen—generally the stone shingle of wide burns, and where it would not set fire to anything else—and then she would put her little iron plate on top of the glowing embers and grill the strips of venison meat or fish the mysterious people left for them. Before the Clan left, they removed all the charred wood, put it in the burn to be washed downstream, and threw away the stones they had used to act as sides for their fire. Then they covered the burned patch with either turf or gravel and felt very proud about leaving no trace.

They drank water from the burns, but always with care, picking a little waterfall section so that the water was free from dirt or sediment.

In this manner they journeyed on until they saw a large loch in the distance, surrounded by high mountains, and with woods along its shores. They could smell a fresh, salt smell in the air and Clare said that the loch might lead to the sea.

The trees were all green with the new leaves of spring, the sun shone, the air was fresh and cool, and on the hillsides whin bushes were bright yellow with flowers. Sometimes they had to push through these or make detours to avoid them.

'I don't remember bushes being as thick as this at home,' said Clare.

'No,' agreed Michael. 'It's harder too to get through the woods because there are so many old branches and low bushes and other plants.'

'I think it's because we haven't seen any sheep and only a handful of deer,' said Gavin. He pulled out his beloved notebook and consulted it again. 'Yes, here we are .... Uncle Fergus told me that when the sheep came in large numbers in our own time they ate all the grass, the young trees when they were shoots, and all the flowers. That's one of the reasons why the hillsides are mainly bare of trees. The deer do the same there too.

'But it's different here. Everything gets a chance to grow and it's much nicer.'

'Much harder to get through, you mean,' said Mot, as he tried in vain to push through a large copse of hazel trees, gorse and high heather.

They eventually worked their way down to the shore.

'Clare!' shouted Gavin. 'I've just had an idea.'

'What?' asked Clare, trying to climb over a fallen tree trunk.

'There's so much whin around with its yellow flower that it might be like a yellow wall. The sunset looked like our yellow wall as the Fianne told us to travel westwards, but this stuff is *also* yellow.'

'Yes, that's true,' said Michael, wrapping his plaid tightly round him and pushing with his back against the gorse so that he didn't feel the prickles so much.

'You might well be right,' agreed Mot. 'But there's no harm in having two yellow walls. Anything which helps get us home is welcome, as far as I'm concerned.'

They pushed on in silence for a time, concentrating on getting over logs covered in mosses and other plants, dodging banks of hazel and gorse, until they were near the shore of the loch.

'This looks like it,' said Clare. 'But don't push through to the open shore just yet. Let's take it carefully and look around first.'

She stopped just inside a line of trees and juniper bushes and gazed up and down the shore.

'I wonder which way we're supposed to go?' she said. 'Up or down? This looks like a long loch.'

'I know,' whispered Gavin. 'We could wander for miles and still be going in the wrong direction.'

'A conference is called for,' said Michael. 'We should all sit down, and make a plan.'

'A seat would be a good idea, anyway,' said Mot. 'I'm tired.' He perched on a log, swinging his legs and looking at the others. Clare would soon make a decision.

They were all busy with their own thoughts for a few seconds, when Clare suddenly sprang up and pointed silently up the loch shore. The boys, galvanised into action by her sudden movement, also stood up and followed her pointing hand. She was good at this, indicating things without saying a word.

A column of what looked like smoke rose steadily into the clear air from a spot near a little bay about a mile away.

'Let's take a look at that,' said Clare. 'But carefully. Check you have all got your feathers. Follow me in single file.'

She began to walk carefully up the loch shore, but still staying within the tree-line whenever possible. Some mallard ducks splashed out from a little bay and flew away squawking noisily.

'Drat!' exclaimed Clare. 'That might give us away. Go carefully now.'

She continued to move slowly and silently up the lochside.

Then, from a tree somewhere in front of them, a cuckoo called loudly.

CHAPTER XIII

Deirdre-of-the-Sorrows

THE Clan clutched one another in glee and Clare did a little dance. Mot, Michael and Gavin pummelled one another with their fists in mock relief. A cuckoo! They were another step on the way home.

Then, from all around them, came the sound of more cuckoos, that lovely, far-off call of a Highland spring, a call telling of the cold days coming to an end even though the snow still lingered on the high peaks; of the fresh green grass and budding trees and of sunlight and warmth.

'Come on,' said Clare. 'Onward!'

The boys were all cheerful.

'I think things might be going our way at last,' said Gavin.

'Not before time,' grumbled Mot. 'It's all right for you. I was grabbed by a witch, put under a spell and tied up and locked in a hut.'

Michael chuckled: 'It can't have been fun.' But his face clouded a little. 'It must have been frightening ... ,' he added.

'Too true,' said Mot with such feeling that Michael and Gavin glanced at him for a second and then saw by his face that it had, indeed, been an alarming and terrifying experience.

'Never mind, Mot,' said Clare. 'You did well and we got you out.'

'I know,' said Mot. 'It was great to see the Fianne with their weapons and hear their war horns. They weren't long in shifting the Cailleach Bheur.'

'No,' agreed Michael. 'I'm glad she's gone for ever.'

They continued to walk in single file through the woods and along the loch shore. The day smiled. They could hear curlews trilling on the moors and see the black and white feathers and red beaks of oyster catchers dotting around the shingle and hear their piercing calls as they flew low over the water, getting all fussed and bothered about nothing.

'Wait there a moment,' said Clare, waving the boys in behind a large boulder while she crawled out on to the shingle and looked up the shore to where she could still see the column of smoke. This time it was very much closer and had broken up and was eddying around as if a new fire had settled down.

She crawled back: 'We're quite near now. We'd better go very carefully. Keep in behind me and stop when I raise my hand.'

They continued to move cautiously through the trees and then came to the top of a little rise where there was a grove of oak trees, with grassy spaces between them. Down below was a large, open hollow with a little burn running through it. In the middle was a kind of shelter or bower made of branches and covered in bracken, moss and leaves. A little fire burned outside it and two men squatted beside it. They looked as if they had been hunting because a deer lay dead beside them and deer skins were drying on trestles made of branches not far from the shelter.

The men were red-haired and, like the small dark men, their hair was roughly cut in a straight line across their forehead. They wore tartan plaids like the Clan, but their tartan did not have red as the main colour, but brown and green.

It fitted into the landscape, Clare thought, as she lay behind a tree watching them. That was true of their own colour, too; it was not a bright colour, but soft and muted, not unlike the reds and browns you see in leaves in the autumn. The men wore sporrans on their hips.

They began to cut up deer meat with a sharp knife and to lay it in strips on an iron plate which they placed across the stones so that the flames gathered underneath.

'What do you think, Clare,' whispered Michael. 'Shall we go down? It looks okay.'

Clare glanced to where Mot and Gavin were also hidden behind trees. 'What do you two think?'

Mot and Gavin both gave nods of assent.

'There may be more people around,' Clare said. 'That shelter has room for three or four of them.'

Gavin tapped her on the arm and pointed: 'There's another shelter further over in the trees, just beside that big oak tree. Look!'

Clare could see a second shelter. Just behind it she thought she could make out a third.

'Let's go down,' she said. 'If we don't take a risk we'll never find the Princess Deirdre. Put your ptarmigan feathers at the front of your bonnets. Make them obvious.'

The boys checked their feathers were firmly fixed and then Clare stood up and walked clear of the trees. 'Keep hidden for the moment,' she said over her shoulder at the boys.

The men caught sight of her and both leapt up. She held up her hand in the ancient salute she was now so accustomed to and looked down at them.

They eyed her closely. When they saw her green dress and gold headband and the cluster of white feathers she held in her hand, they began to talk quickly to one another.

Then, like the Fianne, they knelt down on one knee.

Clare moved down towards them and the boys followed her, after a moment's hesitation. On seeing the boys, the men leapt to their feet again and looked at them with surprise. They then indicated to each other that the boys had ptarmigan feathers like Clare.

'Who are you?' Clare asked.

One of the men spoke: 'I am Naoise, of the house of Uisneach. Who are you?'

'I am the Princess Clare,' said Clare. She felt it was all right to call herself that as it was the term used by everyone so far. It seemed to go down well.

'My brothers and I are journeying back to our own people and our own land and we are seeking the Princess Deirdre.'

Naoise looked closely at her: 'This is my brother Ardan. Who are these boys with you and what do you seek of Deirdre?'

Clare said: 'They are called Michael, Gavin and Mot. They are my brothers and a friend.'

Naoise seemed to relax as he examined them. He said: 'You're carrying the magic feathers of the ptarmigan. This means you will come to no harm with us and you will cause us no harm. That is good.'

Clare said: 'We wish no harm to anyone. We only want to return to our home. We have had many adventures and escaped evil creatures. We have met the small dark men and the warriors of the Fianne.'

Naoise gasped: 'You met the Fianne? You were fortunate indeed. Come, sit beside the fire and tell us of your journeyings.'

So the Clan sat on the grass near the fire. While Naoise and Ardan listened intently, they told their story all over again. The men gave little gasps at the most exciting parts and Ardan reached for his knife when they told him of the Cailleach Bheur. He put it down again when they said she had been drowned, vanishing into the magic spring.

Gavin took out his notebook and read the prophecy and the tasks, making a good job of it, reading it out boldly. But when he had finished he rather spoiled the effect by briskly saying: 'We've managed five—the magic spring, the harper, the horn, the golden wall and the cuckoo.' He said it in such a matter-of-fact fashion that Clare almost giggled.

She regained her dignity quickly:

'We were told by Conn, the leader of the Fianne and victor of many battles, that we should travel to the west, through the golden wall of the sunset to find the Princess Deirdre. She may be the maid forlorn of our prophecy and thus she would help us.'

Naoise nodded his head. He looked very sad. 'That is true, oh Princess,' he said. 'Deirdre is indeed forlorn. She and I ran away from the court of an evil king in a land far from here called Erin. We were to be married. Now the king has sent a friend called Fergus to find us and has promised us many riches and our safety if we return to his land.

'I do not want to do that because I fear him and I know he wishes to marry the Princess Deirdre himself. You see, when Deirdre was a child, her parents died. The king looked after her for many years and she believes she is doing wrong if she does not return and confront him, to free herself of any obligation to him. She feels she can only truly be free if she does that. But it is also true that she will be very sad to leave this lovely place.'

Ardan added: 'We have built bowers here in Glen Etive. The sun shines. We have many cattle and we go hunting in the hills and glens with our spears and our dogs. We have all been happy.

'But our days are coming to an end. Soon the royal barge of King Connochbar of Ulster will arrive here and Fergus will take us to the Stone of Farewell on the shores of Loch Etive and we will step on board from that stone and never see these green glens again.'

Both men looked sad now.

Clare said: 'But I do not understand! Tell Fergus that you will *not* go! You must stay if you are so happy? Why not marry Deirdre here?'

Naoise said: 'There is a prophecy—a *geas* as it is known in our tongue—that she and I must return. It is ordained. So we will go. But our happiness is not as it was, and a cloud has come over our sun. We love this land called Alba and do not want to leave it.'

The boys listened carefully and then Michael said: 'Where is the Princess Deirdre now? Can we speak with her?'

Naoise said nothing for a moment and then a curtain at the entrance to the bower parted and out stepped a tall woman.

'I am Deirdre. What do you want of me?'

She had long hair as black as a raven, skin as white as snow, lips red as the rowan berry and her eyes were green as moss in springtime. She wore a long dress of a yellow or golden colour and had a kind of tartan shawl around her shoulders with a broad band of white on the hem. On her forehead was a gold band very similar to Clare's.

She wore currans on her feet, and the ends of the thongs were tipped with gold. Around her waist she wore a belt of green, set with jewels.

The woman looked at them all for a moment and then said in a voice as soft as the murmuring of a far-off burn, 'I am Deirdre. What do you want of me?'

CHAPTER XIV

Howls in the Night

CLARE thought later that they had never had such a wonderful adventure as this. They poured out their story to Deirdre, as they had to Naoise. She listened gravely and then took them to her own bower.

It was like being inside a huge green tent, Gavin thought to himself, as he looked around. It was made of large branches which formed the frame. Green ferns and rushes had been woven into it to make the roof and these were renewed when they withered.

The floor was of packed clay, reddish in colour, and so were the lower walls. Other branches and deer hides separated the bower into two rooms. One of these was Deirdre's bedroom, and the floor and part of the walls were covered in the down of birds and there were many, soft, deer skins scattered around.

There was a little window or gap in one of the walls and Mot went to that and looked through.

'Goodness!' he exclaimed. 'The river is just below here. I could fish in that pool from here, without going outside.'

Deirdre smiled. 'That is right,' she said. 'I sometimes do that. Naoise and Ardan make rods of birch branches and we have caught salmon from here. Naoise's other brother, Aluinn, makes hooks from little pieces of metal and flies from old feathers and bits of wool.'

Gavin also went to the little window and looked out. He could see the River Etive running over the rocks, a lively river with many little waterfalls and deep pools, and to his right he could see the broad waters of the loch.

The sun shone on the green hills and woods, little snow patches high up in the mountains glistened, and the cuckoos continued to call, a magical sound.

Gavin heaved a sigh of happiness. It was all so perfect— the river, the loch, the hills, the sheltering bower and their new friends.

They talked far into the night, but before they drifted off to sleep in an empty bower into which Naoise had placed more deer skins, Deirdre put her head round the door and said: 'I will wake you very early. You must see the sun rise, red and golden. It will be a good omen for you all. Sleep well until then.'

The children looked at one another. 'Why does she want us to see the sunrise?' asked Clare. 'What's so special about that? Well, we should do as she asks, I suppose. It's only polite. She's been so wonderful and kind to us.'

Gavin said: 'Seeing the sun rising is nothing new to us. Do you remember when we were trying to save the white stag*? We all went up the hill and saw the sun rise.'

'That's right,' remembered Mot. 'I remember the colours and how quiet it was in the night. We were a bit tired the next day, though.'

'Yes,' said Michael. 'It was a great night and saving the white stag was a great adventure. But Mot's right. We were tired because we had not slept properly.'

'Well, there's a sensible answer to that,' said Clare. 'Let's get all the sleep we can now. Morning will come soon enough.'

They lay down on the deer skins in their warm plaids and put their rucksacks beside them. Soon there was nothing to be heard but the steady breathing of the children, the sigh of the night wind in the trees, and the chuckling of the river as it made its way into the loch.

Late in the night Gavin woke up for a brief moment. All was dark, but he could make out the sleeping figures of the other children. Through a little gap in the walls he could see the night

*See *The White Stag Adventure* by Rennie McOwan (Saint Andrew Press)

sky, blue-black in colour with its little stars faintly twinkling.

He turned over and was just about to go to sleep again when he heard an odd noise. It was like a far-off dog barking. Then came a kind of howl, like a wolf, eerie and frightening. He sat up and listened intently, but he didn't hear it again. He began to think it was his imagination and stopped himself waking Clare to tell her about it.

He lay down again and fell fast asleep, and didn't hear the second howl which came some minutes later. It was just as well, because the second howl, menacing and more dangerous, was much, much nearer.

CHAPTER XV

The Face of the Sun

'WHAT, what? ... what is it?' muttered Clare as a hand tapped her shoulder and she awoke from a deep sleep. 'Where am I?' She sat up and looked around. Then she remembered she was not back in the old farm near Callander, but centuries back in a different world.

Clare felt a momentary feeling of panic and then got a grip on herself. She recognised Deirdre's face and saw that Deirdre was smiling.

'Wake up, Clare,' whispered Deirdre. 'It is still very early in the morning, but I want you all to see the sun rising. Naoise has made you a special present for your journey, but he is still working on it and will give it to you later. Waken the boys and then come to my bower.'

'I will, oh Deirdre,' said Clare, who was finding it difficult *not* to speak in the style of long ago. She smiled to herself and then gave the boys a shake.

There was much grumbling and protesting and Michael said sleepily: 'Go away, Clare ... I'll get up in a minute.'

Clare poked him in the ribs with her toe until he wriggled around and eventually sat up.

'Go out to the river and wash,' she said.

'Wash?' asked Mot incredulously.

'Yes,' said Clare. 'Wash! You know ... that's the thing you do occasionally and only when you're *made* to.'

There was no stopping Clare when she got into one of her 'I'm-in-charge' moods, so the sleepy boys tip-toed down to the river through the ferns, heather and grasses still wet with dew and splashed their faces and hands with water.

It was still dark when they rejoined Clare and they they all went to Deirdre's bower. She was wearing a hooded tartan cloak over her dress and carried a wooden staff which had carvings on it.

'Come!' Deirdre said. 'We are going to the *grianan*, the sunny place,' and she led the way across the heather towards a little hill. She seemed to know the way and walked steadily, but occasionally the boys tripped and fell in the heather. They muttered under their breath until Deirdre told them to stay silent.

'This is a sacred place,' she explained. 'Our ancestors have worshipped here for many centuries and we must be quiet when we stand here or we will not sense their spirits and they will not be able to help us.'

Deirdre walked on a tiny path which led to the foot of a knoll. Even in the half-dark the boys could see that there was a tall stone, like a pillar, on the top of the mound.

'Follow me,' said Deirdre. 'Stand close to me.'

They all reached the top of the small mound and panted a little. They had not eaten anything yet and they had only slept for part of the night, yet Deirdre seemed as fresh as ever.

She smiled a lot when she looked at the children and yet her face seemed sad at other times.

'You have become soft in your land,' Deirdre commented quietly. 'You cannot walk long distances without food and without becoming tired. Naoise, Aluinn, Ardan and I can all walk for a long time with no ill effects.'

'But we *are* getting better at it,' said Clare. 'We have come a long way from the Corrie-of-the-Goblins.'

'Yes,' said Gavin. 'We seem to be able to stand cold and wet better and we are getting fitter.' Mot and Michael nodded in agreement.

'That is good,' Deirdre said. 'For you have a long journey to undertake and you will face many perils before you return to your own people. Watch now what I do and copy me, and at all times be silent or talk only in whispers.'

She walked to the base of the tall stone and placed her palm firmly against it and then indicated that the children should do the same. She stood motionless for a few seconds as if she was trying to hear some sound or signal.

Gavin felt a little tingle of excitement. Clare placed one hand on the stone and held out the other to Gavin. He took it and then held his hand out to Michael, who did the same to Mot. Their bodies began to tingle a little.

Then they heard faint music, like someone playing a harp in the distance and what seemed like far-off voices singing a gentle song, so faint that it merged with the noise of the river running over the rocks and stones and became lost when the night wind set the heather shivering and shaking.

They listened entranced to the music and it cast a kind of golden spell over them so that they stood motionless, one hand on the rock, the other holding the hand of another member of the Clan, and they were all content and happy.

Then the music faded and Deirdre removed her hand and the children did the same.

'What was that?' whispered Clare.

'It made us feel funny, almost asleep ... but happy,' said Gavin.

'Yes,' agreed Michael, 'It seemed like magic, yet we weren't frightened at all.'

Mot nodded his agreement.

'You have heard the People of Quietness,' said Deirdre. 'They are a faery people and live inside green mounds like this one and only play their clarsachs for people they like. Their magic bird, the cuckoo, lives with them inside these mounds all winter. You may never hear them play for you again, but they have given you their protection and have blessed you.'

Clare wasn't quite sure what all of this meant, but any kind of protection was a good idea she thought.

Then Gavin remembered something important. 'Clare!' he exclaimed. 'I thought I heard a dog bark and then howl late last night. I wasn't going to mention it because I couldn't be sure and I might have been mistaken. It might only have been the wind.'

Deirdre swung round: 'What!?' she cried. 'You heard a howl? When was this ... and what exactly did you hear?' She seemed alarmed and her smile had gone.

Gavin explained it all again. At the second telling it seemed very slight and unimportant.

'Maybe you dreamt it,' said Michael.

'Yes, that would be it,' said Mot, in a relieved tone. 'A dream.'

Deirdre's voice sounded troubled. 'If you hear it again, you *must* tell me,' she whispered. 'That is very important. There are magic hounds in these mountains who once belonged to the Cailleach Bheur. They are evil. You must tell me instantly if you hear anything again so that Naoise, Aluinn and Ardan can make ready their spears.

'You see, the dogs were here many years ago, but we thought they were hunting elsewhere, far beyond the mountains called the Five Sisters and the green glen where the sacred waterfalls lie.

'Come! This makes it all the more important that we see the sun rise. You have heard the People of Quietness and now have much protection around you, but you will need more.'

She went to the other side of the stone and sat down on a smaller boulder and gazed to where the sky on the far side of distant mountains was becoming lighter. But before she did so, she stood behind the stone.

'What are you doing, Deirdre?' asked Clare.

'I am making sure we and the stone are in line with that notch on the far off mountains. It marks where the sun will come up,' Deirdre said.

They all fell silent for a few minutes as the sky grew lighter.

Then a green line appeared in the sky in the notch, followed a few seconds later by a red line. Then the sun came up, golden and wonderful, and sent long rays on to the hill and scattered the night-time shadows.

The children forgot the need to be silent and all gave a little cheer and then stopped as if they had been silenced by a giant's hand.

The sky was becoming yellow and orange with little purple clouds floating around and red sections where the sun and the clouds were mixed up. Before the stupefied eyes of the children, the clouds and the sun began to form the shape of a giant face.

It seemed to be that of a woman with long, golden hair. They could see her eyes of purple-blue, her face shining in the sunlight, her teeth sparkling like new clouds in spring and her lips crimson like clouds in a sunset. Her face grew and spread until it covered most of the eastern sky. She seemed almost to be looking down on Deirdre and the children.

The Face seemed to smile and, like the People of Quietness, it filled them with a feeling of happiness, of well-being. They were not afraid.

They looked up, mesmerised, at this glorious and beautiful face smiling down at them. Then Deirdre suddenly sank down on one knee and bowed her head.

Clare, Michael, Mot and Gavin quickly looked at one another and then did the same. It seemed right and fitting to do so.

The golden light covered them all for a few seconds, making them blink, bathing them in warmth, and when they looked up again the face had gone, the sun was high in the sky and the day had fully begun.

'Deirdre,' said Clare in a trembling voice. 'Who on earth was that?'

CHAPTER XVI

Bride of the Spring

DEIRDRE stretched out her arms and seemed to gather the children together.

'That was Bride,' she said. 'She is a goddess and very powerful. She appears with the sun and the warmth of the spring. When we hear the cuckoo call we know that she is with us, but this is the first time I have seen her face in the sun. That is indeed strange.'

The children were still silent with awe. 'She had a beautiful face,' whispered Clare. 'It made me want to reach out and touch her.'

'Yes,' said Gavin. 'It was shining and lovely and I felt as if I was under a spell.'

Michael nodded, too bemused to say anything.

Mot grunted: 'Let's not get too soppy,' he said.

When Clare glared at him, he hurriedly added: 'Well ... yes, it was special all right. I was frightened at first and then I felt very happy.'

Deep down he was still very puzzled and he didn't know what to think. That great, golden, smiling, welcoming face in the sky was still in his mind.

'We should go back now,' said Deirdre. 'The morning is well advanced and you will all be very hungry.'

She led the way downhill and across the moor. When they reached the River Etive again, some oyster catchers flew up, piping noisily, their red beaks and black and white feathers clearly seen.

Deirdre laughed. 'They are always making a fuss,' she said. 'We love to see them. They are also known as the birds of Bride because when they come here from the seashores we know that winter has passed and spring is here or on the way.'

She was silent for a while as they tramped back, the morning sun warm on their backs.

Suddenly she stopped, turned and spoke to the children: 'I have been thinking about Bride appearing in the sky before us,' she said. 'That must mean something *very* special. I think it is a good omen and she is offering you her special protection. If so, that might mean you are going to face great danger. You must all be careful and as prepared as you can be for your journey.

'I think you should rest today and travel tomorrow. You can explore the land close to the bowers, but no further. Remember, Gavin thought he heard a dog howl and that must be taken into account.'

Deirdre led them back to the bowers where they ate a huge breakfast of barley scones, eggs, grilled meat and a kind of porridge. They drank milk out of flagons made from the horns of cows.

'What shall we do for the rest of the day?' asked Clare lazily, as she stretched back on the soft deer skins.

'Let's just play around beside the river,' said Mot. 'We've done a lot of walking. It's very warm. I wouldn't mind a swim.'

'That's a good idea,' said Michael. 'The loch will be very cold though and I remember Uncle Fergus saying we shouldn't swim in lochs except at the edge because the cold water further out can give you cramp.'

Gavin had been lying full length on his back. He turned over and said, 'We shouldn't really swim in any of the pools in the river—it will disturb the fish when Naoise and the others are trying to catch them. Why don't we find a pool in one of the burns running into the river?'

'Good idea!' said Clare. 'Let's do that then.'

She went off to tell Deirdre of their plans and returned saying that Deirdre thought it would be a suitable thing to do. However, Deirdre warned them about beings called water horses which lived in the lochs and sometimes caught and drowned children. So the burn was most definitely a better idea.

They wandered upstream, happy in the morning sunlight, feeling energetic once more as a result of the huge breakfast, until they came to a little pool, about two feet deep and the length of two average size rooms. It had large rocks at the side and a little waterfall tumbled into the pool at one end. It was fringed by birches and the water flowed out again in a gap between the rocks. It was deep beside the fall, shallow at the other end.

'We could dam that,' said Gavin, pointing to the gap.

'So we could,' said Michael. 'It would make the pool deeper so we could get more swimming strokes.'

'Yes,' agreed Clare. 'This is a good place, enough room to swim without being dangerous or too deep or fast flowing.'

Mot added: 'I'll supervise the building work.' He sank back in the heather and started to go to sleep again until Clare gave him a kick with her toe. 'Everyone's got to work,' she said.

'We're supposed to be resting,' protested Mot.

'It doesn't matter,' said Clare. 'We're going to have fun here. It'll only take a few minutes to build a dam.'

The protesting Mot got up and joined the others in collecting large stones and lumps of turf prised from the bank further up the burn.

Then Gavin and Michael jumped into the water beside the gap. It was only just up to their knees, but it was cold to start with and made them gasp.

They lodged boulders into the gap and on top of the stones at the side of the gap until they had made a kind of thick wall. The flow of the water was reduced to a trickle through gaps in the stones.

'This is great,' said Mot, forgetting he had refused to help.

'Look!' said Clare. 'The water is rising all right.'

'Quick!' she added. 'Get that turf pushed into the gaps on top of the wall.'

They all got very messy pushing the grass, heather and brown peaty turf into the holes, but the flow of water slackened and almost stopped and the level of the pool rose.

After a time the burn began to flow over the top of the wall, but the level had risen in the pool inside by about a foot.

'This pool is deeper beside the waterfall,' said Clare. 'We don't have swimming costumes, but we can swim in our tunics. It's very like a costume anyway, under our plaids.'

She stood beside the pool, swept her hair back, held her nose and jumped in beside the waterfall, sending a shower of water over the boys. They shouted insults and then they too jumped in, with the exception of Gavin who hesitated on the bank for a moment.

He watched Clare swimming up the little pool, doing the breaststroke. He thought she looked like a swimming frog, her tanned arms and legs looking pale in the dark water. She could swim well though.

Gavin wasn't much of a swimmer so he gingerly stepped into a shallow part and sat down in the water.

'It's better jumping in,' said Mot. 'You get the cold over with quickly.'

'Yes, but it isn't that bad,' said Michael. 'We must be quite hardened to the outdoors by now. We'd never have coped with this quite so well back home.'

'True,' said Gavin. 'We're all pretty fit now and our legs and arms are getting very tanned.'

Clare pulled herself out of the pool and sat on a rock, basking in the sun.

The boys began to smack the surface of the pool with the palms of their hands, sending showers of water over her. She made a face and moved away a little.

She was very happy. The pool was clean and not dangerous. The water was refreshing and the sun kept their heads and shoulders warm. A little breeze stirred the birches and kept the flies away. Down below she could see the River Etive running into the long loch and the green bowers where Deirdre and Naoise stayed. She could see two figures beside the river, probably Aluinn and Ardan, who would be fishing for salmon.

All around were big, blue mountains and she could see two far-off pointed peaks with a deep notch or gap in between. She thought that would be the route they would take the next day on their perilous journey.

She shivered for a moment, and then was happy again. If she remembered little else, she was sure that all her life she would remember this—the spring sun in the Highlands, the clean scent of the trees and grass, the splash of the burn water, sounds and noises which she felt would live for ever.

She spread out her plaid and cloak and lay down in the sun. The water was already drying on her. She drifted off to sleep.

* * *

Clare awoke with a start. Gavin was shaking her and Mot and Michael were looking on with serious expressions. They had their plaids and currans back on.

'Clare! Clare!' said Gavin urgently. 'Wake up!'

'What is it?' she said, very annoyed at having her lovely sleep interrupted.

'Gavin's seen a wolf or a dog,' said Michael.

'What?' said Clare, startled.

'Yes,' said Gavin. 'You were sleeping and Michael and Mot were playing in the burn. I just wandered off to that big rock over there. I climbed on top of it and could see a long way down another glen. It was then I saw it.'

'Saw it! Saw *what?*' demanded Clare. 'What did you see?'

'A kind of wolf or dog,' stated Gavin. 'It was a long way off, but it looked black against the ground, not red-brown like a deer, and it scrambled on to the top of a mound and sat there.

'It didn't see me, and the wind was blowing from it towards me so it couldn't scent me.'

'Well?' demanded Clare 'What did it do. Did it go away after that?'

'No,' said Gavin. 'It just sat there with its ears up and then it was joined by another. It was big though, bigger than any dog I've ever seen. And it was definitely black in colour.'

'What did you do then?' asked Clare, hurriedly, pulling on her dress and plaid.

'I wriggled back down and came straight back here and told Mot and Michael,' said Gavin. 'Then we woke you.'

'Good thinking!' said Clare. 'Quick, we'd better get back down to the bowers. We may not have a lot of time. I suppose we could be over-reacting—they may just be ordinary wolves or dogs.'

'I know,' said Gavin. 'But remember the prophecy. We have to see the dogs that kill.'

He quoted the prophecy again:

> 'You must climb the sacred hill,
> You must see the dogs that kill,
> You must seek the hidden tree,
> Or lost forever you will be.'

'Perhaps the faery knoll with the standing stone where we saw Bride was the sacred hill,' said Michael, in a tone of excitement.

'No, it can't have been,' said Clare. 'Deirdre would have told us. It was a special hill, true—a sacred hill—but not ours.'

'Yes, that's probably right,' said Gavin.

Mot nodded his agreement.

95

'Let's get back down to the bowers,' said Clare again. 'We can do all our discussing down there and ask Deirdre and Naoise what we should do.

'Right ... no more dallying. It may be nothing, but if it really is the dogs that kill, then we shouldn't hang around here.'

They hurried downhill, pushing through the birches and were glad to see the foot of the glen beneath them, the green bowers and a slim column of blue smoke arising from a fire. They could see the sun shining on the spears Aluinn and Ardan had leaned against a tree and that eased their minds.

They were not without help.

But it was not a moment too soon.

From the hillside behind them came a long howl, followed a moment later by another. It echoed among the rocks. From the camp below, Deirdre, Naoise, Aluinn and Ardan came running out of the bowers and from the side of the river. They gazed upwards startled, as the children ran panting towards them.

'It's the dogs! It's the dogs!' gasped Clare.

Another two howls rent the air behind them and before their startled eyes two huge wolf-like shapes gathered on a large boulder just above their camp.

As they looked up at them, it seemed that the black dogs grew larger and larger, the howls louder and louder, until the whole glen seemed to reel with the fearsome, terrifying noise.

The children looked up in horror at their huge red eyes, their glistening teeth, their large black heads and shoulders and huge jaws wet with saliva. The snarls and howls made their heads birl. They were all petrified as the dogs grew in size until they were like a black cloud over the sun, the snarling faces becoming even more evil.

Before the other children could stop him, Gavin picked up two pieces of wood and charged uphill towards the dogs.

... the dogs grew in size until they were like a black cloud over the sun, the snarling faces becoming even more evil.

CHAPTER XVII

The Hidden Tree

LATER on Gavin was to say he didn't know what made him do it. He had just looked up at the fierce, giant-like, snarling dogs and then he had looked for some kind of stick to defend himself.

At his feet he saw a tiny bush, looking rather like gorse or whin, and then he remembered something he had written in his notebook long ago.

'It's juniper!' his frantic mind said. 'The plant-like tree which frightens away evil things.'

He remembered Uncle Fergus telling him that in the past nearly every tree in a wood had a different kind of spirit attached to it, some good, some bad—as well as the different types of wood being used for different things, like furniture, handles for weapons, for wheels or arrows.

All this had raced through his mind in a few seconds and he acted so quickly he almost forgot to be afraid. He simply ran uphill. Later he thought it was as if his legs belonged to someone else. The snarling from the dogs grew louder and they crouched down as if they would leap from the rock on to him.

He held up the handful of juniper branches and leaves and an astonishing thing happened.

The dogs reared up and bayed at the sky, their bellowing bark echoing from the nearby rocks and along the loch-side.

Meanwhile, down below, Naoise, Aluinn and Ardan had snatched up their spears and were also running up the hill. Clare, Michael and Mot, meantime, armed themselves with stones and sticks.

Gavin waved the branches and leaves again, flourishing them in front of him as he stood at the foot of the rock and looked up at the dogs. Later on, he was shocked at what he had done because it might have all gone wrong.

'They might have leapt down and tried to kill me,' he said to Clare, when it was all over. 'I don't know what made me do it.'

The dogs continued to snarl and bark, but they also shrank back and, like the Cailleach Bheur, they seemed to shrink in size until they were like normal dogs. Although they still stood on the rock howling, the tone had lost much of its anger and menace.

Gavin walked up towards them, still brandishing the branches. To his astonishment, the two dogs gave one last despairing howl and then leapt down from the back of the rock and on to the moorland.

They began to run over the moor and soon disappeared over a heather mound. Gavin caught one further glimpse of them as they crossed another hillock, and then they vanished from his sight.

He sank down on to the ground, his legs trembling.

When he next looked up he was surrounded by an admiring crowd.

Naoise and Deirdre looked down at him with amazement. Clare kept patting him on the shoulder and Mot and Michael sat down beside him, speechless for a few minutes because they couldn't think what to say.

It had all been too terrifying, dramatic, sudden and awful ... and then the dogs had vanished.

'What on earth did you do that for, Gavin?' cried the bewildered Clare.

'It's juniper,' explained Gavin, still clutching a handful.

Naoise and Deirdre gasped.

'How do you know of such things?' asked Naoise. Aluinn and Ardan, who stood behind him, clutching bows and arrows, craned forward to hear Gavin's answer.

'We know of these things,' said Deirdre. 'We know that in our land there are spirits in the trees, but we did not know juniper grew in this little glen. It is a magic tree.'

Gavin nodded. 'Oh Naoise,' he said, 'in our land we have an uncle and he knows a lot about your customs from reading and studying books. He gave me a list of all trees and the spirits who were supposed to live in them.

'I copied them into my little notebook. I remembered that juniper was special and gave protection against evil.

'I was very afraid and I'm not sure why I did it, but it seemed the right thing to do at the time.'

Naoise looked approvingly at him. 'Perhaps it was several things,' he said. 'You all have the ptarmigan feathers. That would give you some protection. You saw Bride in the sunrise and Ossian said he would help you. All of that perhaps gives you courage.

'The juniper would be just enough on top of that to frighten the dogs, but perhaps not by itself.'

The children began to recover themselves.

'Let's see this old plant,' said Clare. Gavin held out parts of a little bush which looked like an evergreen or a small yew tree. They all examined it with interest.

'I can remember some other things about it,' said Gavin. 'Its smoke is almost invisible and it was used when people didn't want fires to be seen.'

'That is true,' said Naoise. 'But we don't use it much here because it is rare in these glens. It was truly an act of good fortune that you saw some here.'

'What else does it do?' asked Michael, recovering his voice.

'Well,' said Gavin, thinking hard. 'Its berries were used as medicine and they also made a kind of drink, and the wood was burned on the doorsteps of houses at Hallowe'en to keep people safe from harm. I can't remember any more.'

'You've done pretty well even remembering all that,' said Mot.

They began to relax, sitting down on the heather.

Clare looked around her. The loch and the hills still looked beautiful in the sunlight and there was a feeling of some great threat having been taken away from them.

'Let us go back down now,' said Naoise. 'We must make preparations for your journey tomorrow. You will be safer now the dogs have gone, but you still have to pass through a land of high mountains and wide straths and deep glens. There may be other enemies there.'

'Yes,' said Deirdre. 'You must eat and sleep well. We must part soon, but I will always remember you. When Naoise and I return to Ireland, we will ask our druids, the men who know about magic things, to try to protect you from afar.'

So they all trooped downhill and spent the rest of the day resting on the deer skins, and sorting out their little sacks for the journey the next day.

They sat silently for a time as the evening sun began to set, throwing long shadows on to the loch and up the glens. They could see little groups of red deer appearing on the grassy flat sections beside the loch where they came to graze in the evening.

Then Clare had a thought. She sat bolt upright: 'We're all stupid!' The boys looked at her. 'We've achieved another of our tasks,' she said. 'The dogs that kill! We saw them. They would have killed us, but for Gavin. Now they're defeated and have gone for ever.'

'That's right,' said Michael. 'Only two to go—the hidden tree and the sacred hill. We'll need to think about that and work out what we do.'

Mot began to hop up and down with excitement.

'What is it, Mot?' asked Clare in exasperation. 'Sit down! I'm tired and I was comfortable until you started leaping around.'

Mot continued to leap up and down. 'It's not two, it's *one!*' he cried. 'It's *one!*'

'How do you mean "one"?' asked Gavin.

'Yes, one!' said Mot. 'The juniper is your hidden tree. Don't you see? Naoise said it was rare here. We never saw it before. It was *hidden* in that sense. You found it and used it to defeat the dogs.'

Clare thought for a moment. 'You might be right,' she said slowly. 'It would certainly fit.'

Gavin and Michael nodded in agreement. 'Yes, it does sound right,' Gavin said. 'But we can't be sure.'

'No, we can't be sure of anything,' said Clare. 'We couldn't be sure of the horn or the yellow wall, but we kept on on travelling and now we're on our way back home. We won't know for sure that we have completed all the tasks until the last one is done.'

'But how will we know?' asked Mot. 'We don't know what will happen, or how, or even where?'

'Right,' said Michael. 'But we've got to keep plodding on. We don't know how it will come right, but I've got a feeling it will.'

'So have I,' said Gavin.

Clare nodded, but deep down she was not sure. They had a long journey ahead, and then had to find a sacred hill and climb it. She was not sure what was meant by that. Lots of hills, including the faery hills, were sacred. They couldn't climb them all.

However, if they were nearer to where Callander used to be, then that might improve their chances.

By this time it was dark and she lay on the deer skins and looked out at the night sky through a gap in the bower walls. She could see little stars twinkling and that put a little, nagging thought into her mind.

Light! There was something about a sacred hill and light. Someone had said that to her, but she couldn't remember who. She made a mental note to ask Gavin in the morning. Perhaps light, or a light, had something to do with their sacred hill.

Clare had a feeling she was on the right track. She was about to wake Gavin to ask him when a cloud swept over the moon and the stars grew dim. Before she knew it, she was fast asleep.

CHAPTER XVIII

Another Journey

IT took the children many days to travel through the mountains. Once they had to eat part of their dramach, but every now and then they would come across the green, pointed, faery mounds and they would find food put out for them.

They never saw anyone, although they kept a good look out. Clare later thought that perhaps these creatures were invisible. They would hear the roar of a mountain burn, or the croak of a raven, the bark of a red deer stag, or the wind sighing among the crags and sometimes they would think that these noises sounded like the voices of people.

There was certainly someone there. The children would reach the bottom of a faery hill and there they would find a little wooden plate made of birch wood. On it would be berries, or barley scones, or little pieces of venison. Yet the birds or foxes didn't eat it before they got there. It was always untouched.

Gavin tugged Clare by the arm at one of these places: 'Clare!' he whispered, 'I always get the feeling of passing through some kind of door at these places and I feel very happy and have no feeling of fear.'

'I know,' said Clare. 'I feel exactly the same. It's as if we're being welcomed and protected by people we can't see.' Clare was whispering too. These places had a fey feeling about them.

Michael nodded in agreement. 'Perhaps it's our ptarmigan feathers or the pieces of juniper wood we still have?'

'Yes, it might be that,' said Mot. 'Or it could be our new staffs.'

They were all carrying staves or sticks which Naoise had given them. They were very special presents. He had carved them of ash or hazel wood and the top of each stick was carved into the shape of a bird—a peregrine falcon, an eagle, and a ptarmigan. It was very cleverly done.

'I have spent a long time making these, Clare,' said Naoise before they left. 'They are strong and will help you in steep places or if you have to cross deep burns. I have put a bird mark on each so that you will always remember this land and the people you met here.'

Gavin was very moved. 'Thank you, Naoise,' he said. 'We will treasure these sticks and use them well.' Michael and Mot also said thanks.

They stood with their belted plaids comfortably adjusted, their skin rucksacks on their backs and their currans carefully laced on their feet. They had eaten well and Clare, amid protests, had made the boys wash once more.

Deirdre had stood looking at them with tears in her eyes. She gave Clare a hug.

Clare, to hide that she might be about to cry, pretended to look down at her stick. In doing so, she noticed some carving near the foot. She examined it more closely. It was a little oval shape, like a mirror, and just below it was a little cross. Deirdre saw her looking at the little mark and smiled.

'Naoise did that for you all,' she said. 'We are not sure what it means, but it seems wise and good. The little circle is a mirror and to see one's face in a silver mirror or in the water of a still pool can bring good fortune.

'We do not know very much about the little cross, but strange men have come from the far west with teachings of a new religion, a new Faith. I have not heard them, but Naoise has spoken to people who have. They say that these followers of a man called Christ are good men and that one day their Faith will be known all over the land.

'We shall see. In the meantime, I have put one of our magic marks and one of their special marks on your sticks. It can do no harm, and may well give you help.'

Clare nodded gravely. She felt deep down that they might need every bit of help they could get.

'You should go now,' Naoise had said. 'The sun is high up in the sky and you have a long way to travel, back to the hills of the east, back to where your own land might be.'

'Thank you, Naoise,' Gavin said, and he leaned forward and embraced Naoise and then stood back, raising his right hand, palm forward, in the ancient salute. Mot and Michael, both very quiet because they were sad about leaving Naoise, Deirdre, Aluinn and Ardan, did the same. Then they all embraced Deirdre and the brothers.

'Go, Princess,' said Deirdre to Clare, and for a second or two Deirdre looked so sad and forlorn that Clare almost felt that they should all stay.

'I will remember you in the land of Erin across the sea,' said Deirdre. 'The royal barge comes for us soon and we will all travel together. Go in safety and health.'

Deirdre quickly turned and walked back into the bower. Clare thought she could hear her sobbing. Naoise, Aluinn and Ardan also turned and walked away, and the children, by this time all very quiet, set off along the loch shore.

They walked for quite a long time before any of them spoke. When they did finally, they had rounded the shoulder of several hills and the loch was hidden from their view.

Clare let out a sigh. 'Well, that's that,' she said. 'We're on our own now.'

'I know,' said Gavin. 'But we have lots of protection—the feathers, the juniper wood and the carved sticks.'

'True,' said Mot, and they all began to feel better.

'We must keep on going to the east,' said Clare. 'Later in the day we'll try to find a place where we can spend the night. Or we can make one of Gavin's heather beds. They always work well.'

They continued on their journey, following the bottom of the glens and straths. Every now and again they had to wade burns. Their sticks were a help in judging how deep the water was and in helping them against the flow of the current.

Sometimes they found their way barred by steep slopes and had to climb up to the lowest point and then descend again. But they kept going and soon Loch Etive was far behind them.

They stopped sometimes to rest and eat, but most of the time they walked steadily. They were now very fit.

Sometimes they would see red deer on the hills looking down on them, and once they watched an eagle, soaring in great circles above their heads—but they saw no people.

When night came they found caves in the rocks or cut beds of heather and slept soundly, waking up in the early morning to find the heather rocks shining with dew and the morning sun glittering on the hillsides. Sometimes it rained, but they seemed to be tougher and continued on until it stopped and they dried out again.

Three days and three nights passed. The next morning, when they walked to the top of a hill at the head of a glen, they could see a pointed peak in the distance.

'That looks like Ben Ledi,' said Clare, pointing. The others clustered round her and looked carefully at the far off mountain. They all agreed that it did look like Ben Ledi.

Their spirits soared. 'That's great!' said Clare. 'We look as if we're getting near home.'

'Or getting near where home once was,' said Gavin, wryly. 'We don't know what's going to happen when we get there.'

'That's right,' said Mot. 'We might be stuck here for long enough.'

'Or even for ever,' said Michael quietly, putting into words what they had all been thinking, but no one had wanted to say out loud.

'Don't say that,' said Clare, briskly. 'We're going to get back home. Look at what's happened to us so far and we're still here.'

'Well said, Clare,' added Gavin. 'Every time something dreadful happens to us we seem to overcome it. We'll get back all right.'

Mot and Michael nodded approvingly.

'Let's get on,' said Clare. 'I suggest we try and get as far as we can before the light goes.'

They set off again and found a little track, made by deer, which led upwards in easy stages until they found themselves on the broad shoulder of a hill which had blocked the glen they were travelling through.

'Whew!' said Clare, sinking down in the grass and heather at the top. 'That was some climb.'

'Yes,' said Gavin. 'But the little path helped.'

He looked around him. It was beginning to get dark and a little cold. 'We'd better find a shelter for the night, Clare,' he added.

'All right,' Clare agreed. 'Spread out you lot and see if you can find a decent cave.'

The shoulder of the hill was covered in large boulders and the children searched around until they found a large overhanging rock with two other rocks at the side so it made a three-sided shelter. There was room for all of them to lie side by side.

'Let's get cracking before all the light goes,' instructed Clare. 'Gavin! You cut heather. Michael and Mot! You get more stones and cut pieces of turf. We'll build a wall across the entrance.'

Mot gave a mock bow. 'Yes, oh Princess,' he said.

Gavin and Michael chuckled and Clare threw a piece of turf at Mot.

'All right, comedian,' she said. 'Just get on with the work.'

Gavin cut armfuls of heather and piled them up just outside the rocks. Michael and Mot built a little wall across the entrance, high enough to keep a night wind out, but not so high they couldn't step over it. Clare helped them, tugging stones into the gap and then piling lumps of turf on top and in the gap.

When they were finished, Gavin spread the heather over the ground inside their home-made cave and they settled down for the night.

Clare had difficulty in getting to sleep at first. She looked over at the boys. They were sleeping soundly, tightly wrapped up in their plaids.

She looked outside at the night sky. She could see the top of the little wall they had built and then she saw something very strange.

Through a tiny gap in the wall she thought she saw a light, but far away. She sat up and looked over the wall. She could see down the slopes on the far side to where the mountain Ben Ledi soared up to the sky, but by this time they were quite near it.

She wrapped her plaid tightly around her, stepped over the wall and went to the edge of the hill. It was a clear, dry night and she could make out the outline of a glen stretching from their hill towards Ben Ledi. The mountain seemed very close.

But to the side of Ben Ledi and on what seemed to be the lower ground she could see many lights, like the windows of houses twinkling in the distance.

She gasped and hurried back inside the cave and woke the others. Muttering sleepy protests, they gathered outside and stared where Clare was pointing.

'Look!' she said. 'Lights! I told you. It looks like some kind of village.'

The boys looked with great care and then Gavin said: 'You're probably right, Clare. It's strange.'

'Yes, it's obviously not just someone with a fire,' said Michael. 'It's like a whole lot of fires, but they don't look as if they're outside. They look just like lights in a window.'

'Perhaps that is what they are,' said Clare. 'We might be looking down at some kind of village. What did they call them long ago in the Highlands? Do you remember, Gavin?' she asked.

The children had begun to treat Gavin as an expert on all things since the episode with the juniper and the dogs.

'Uncle Fergus told me that groups of houses in the Highlands were once called townships,' Gavin informed them.

'That's it!' exclaimed Clare. 'It's a township. That *must* be it.'

'But why have they all got fires lit as late in the night as this?' asked the puzzled Michael. 'That's a strange thing to do.'

'They're not far away,' said Mot. 'Only a mile or so. Do you think we should go down?'

'Yes,' said Clare. 'But it will need care. We don't want anyone stepping into a hole or falling over a cliff. Still, it's a clear enough night—let's go.'

The boys were astounded. 'But Clare,' said Michael. 'It's half-way through the night.'

'I know,' said Clare. 'But we're very fit these days and we can see in the dark better than we ever could when we were back at home.'

The boys nodded. That was true. It was still dark, but they could pick out a lot of detail which they could never do before. It was almost as if their senses had been heightened to survive the outdoors.

'Yes, I agree we should go down,' said Gavin. 'It must be people and we might be able to get help.'

'I think we should as well,' said Michael. 'Don't forget we've only one more magic task left to complete. Perhaps the people in these houses could tell us about the sacred mountain.'

They discussed it for a few minutes while the moon came up and flooded the ground with a silver light. Gavin bowed to the moon and then stopped, feeling foolish.

'Why did you do that, Gavin?' asked Clare.

'I'm not sure,' he said, a bit embarrassed. 'People did that long ago when the moon came up. Oh, let's get going,' he added to shut them up.

'Well, pack up then,' Clare said.

Soon they were starting off downhill, rejoicing in the clear moonlight, but taking care in the shadows because there were many rocks and holes around.

Then Clare suddenly stopped and let out a gasp. 'Look!' she said.

'What is it?' Gavin asked.

'The lights are going out,' said Clare, amazed.

They all stared downhill.

Before their dumfounded eyes, the lights gradually went out one by one until, once more, all was darkness down below.

CHAPTER XIX

The Hidden Watcher

'STAY together, now,' cautioned Clare as she led the way down-hill. Mot, Michael and Gavin closed up behind her like black shadows. They didn't speak as they crossed the bottom of the glen, keeping their attention on the ground shining in the bright moonlight.

Gavin was lost in his own thoughts when Mot suddenly stopped in front of him and Gavin bumped into him. Mot then crashed into Michael, who jolted into Clare. Mutterings of 'idiot!' … 'watch what you're doing!' … 'look out!' were whispered in a mixture of exasperation and mirth.

But the boys became aware that Clare was standing very still all of a sudden and they quickly fell silent.

Gavin peered round her, but could only see a large pile of boulders, looking very dark and black in the moonlight. 'What is it, Clare?' he asked.

Clare held up her hand for silence. She stood very still for some seconds and then turned and whispered: 'There's someone in these rocks. I saw something move.'

'Are you sure?' asked Michael. 'It might have been a deer.'

'Yes,' whispered Mot. 'Sometimes shadows appear to move at night, but they don't really.'

'I know that,' said Clare. 'It wasn't a deer or a moving shadow, more like a person. Keep you staves handy.'

The boys had been holding their staffs like walking sticks and they now picked them up and held them sideways across their body, ready to deal with trouble.

'Stay where you are,' whispered Clare. She took a couple of paces forward and then said quietly: 'We are travellers from a distant land. We mean you no harm. Who are you? Come out and speak to us.'

The boys exchanged looks in the half-dark and moved more closely to Clare. She motioned them back with her hand and then spoke again, in that formal, almost sing-song, voice she had learned when talking to the Fianne or Naoise.

'I am the Princess Clare,' she said. 'Come out! I will do you no harm.'

There was movement in the shadows, then a small figure stepped out from behind a rock and walked towards Clare. The boys all crouched down, their staves at the ready.

The figure stopped and said: 'I am Angus. I live in this glen, but I will be leaving soon. I mean no one any harm. I come from a land far from here and some people call me a god. Who are you and why are you here in the dark?'

Clare relaxed a little: 'Angus, we are travelling back to our own land. We have to find a sacred hill and then we can return to our own people.

'We know that the hill is called Ben Ledi and we saw many lights down below. We thought we would find people and they would help us, but the lights went out.'

She turned and pointed to Gavin, Michael and Mot. 'These are my brothers and my friend. We are all journeying together. We have had many adventures.'

Angus was silent for a moment and then said: 'Follow me! I have a special task to perform wherever I go. I must make people happy and teach them to love and not to hate.'

He turned and walked back to the boulders and then ducked down and vanished inside a cave. Clare, Michael, Mot and Gavin followed him. After a couple of narrow sections the cave opened out into a large cavern.

'Sit down,' commanded Angus. 'I will light a torch and we

can talk. You have come at a special time because it is now that all the sacred fires of the people are put out and then re-lit. My torch will be the first. These were the lights you saw.

'You can all travel with me. Then you can visit the wood and climb the sacred hill and you should be safe once more.'

The children sat down on the floor of the cave and Angus took out two little stones and struck sparks from them and set fire to a handful of dried moss and grass. Then he lit some pine cones. The shadows moved back and the cave seemed light.

Clare could see that Angus was a boy about the same size as Gavin and Michael. Like them, he wore the belted plaid, but he had long leggings made of deer hide, and like Clare he had a kind of headband on his forehead, almost like a crown. He had blue eyes and long, blond hair.

'I must tell you quickly what is to happen,' he said. 'We have not much time. If we do not light the sacred fires and make the sacred offerings, then the Cailleach Bheur, the Witch-of-the-Storms, or the Dogs-that-Kill might come here. Have you heard of them?'

'Heard of them?' said Mot in excitement. 'We've *fought* them all!'

Angus looked startled. Michael added: 'We met the Cailleach Bheur, but she was destroyed by the Fianne, the warriors of old, and by a burn and then a waterfall which turned into a loch.'

Clare launched into an explanation of their adventures, and Angus listened almost in silence. He occasionally gave a kind of gasp, and once he leapt to his feet and grasped Clare by the hands when he heard about the dogs.

'You have all been brave,' he said. 'You have had much protection, with the juniper and the ptarmigan feathers. These may have saved your lives. But you have been courageous as well. You are like the heroes and heroines of my own land.'

The boys looked at one another with pleasure. No one had ever called them heroes before. Clare noted their pleased expressions and felt that too many compliments were not good for them.

'Well ... yes, that's fine,' she said to Angus, changing the subject. 'But you said we need to hurry. What shall we do? How can we find the sacred hill?'

Angus motioned to them to stand up again and said: 'You have to follow me. You will not see me again after this night, but remember I am called Angus. I do not hate anyone. I am a god of love. But we will have hatred and killing here unless we climb the sacred hill, because the witch or her friends or the dogs will surely come again.'

He turned and led the way out of the cave. Once they were outside, he said gravely: 'You must do exactly as I say. You are almost at the end of your quest. The sacred hill is nearby. But first I will take you through the sacred wood. Remember, you *must* do as I say.'

He turned and looked at each one in turn: 'Do not forget that each time you use your magic talismans to protect you, your juniper and your ptarmigan feathers, they grow weaker and sometimes cannot be used again.

'You need to find new ones. Your feathers and juniper frightened the witch and the black dogs, but they might not do so again. So be careful and follow me.'

The children looked at one another in dismay.

'I thought we would be safe for ever,' said Clare. 'Still, it's as well to know.'

'I'll keep a good look out for more juniper,' said Gavin.

'So will I,' added Michael.

'You never know,' said Mot. 'We might find another ptarmigan and we can get more feathers, but we are among lower mountains now so I think we'll be unlucky.'

Angus turned to them once more: 'Please, no more talking now! I will take you to the magic wood and then we will climb the hill. I will tell you special things and you must remember them because I must leave you soon. But I am fearful just now. We have spent too long here.

'It is no one's fault. I was about to leave when I heard you coming along the path. Sometimes the evil beings of the hills, the witches and their friends, turn themselves into other forms, into hares, deer, wolves, ravens or other people.

'I had to be sure. But we have lost time. Quickly, now! Follow me to the wood. There is no time to spare.'

His tone had such urgency in it that Michael and Mot, who were apt to make jokes at serious times, were totally silent.

Even Gavin shivered a little. He clutched his staff more tightly and looked around at the shining moonlight and the seemingly endless hills.

Then, far off, they all heard an eerie sound. A long drawn out howl rang out followed by another.

'It's the dogs!' cried Angus. 'Quick! Follow me! Don't linger. We have to reach the wood before they come. Quick! Your lives depend on it.'

He turned and ran along a little path. The children glanced at one another and then did the same. Their deer hide shoes seemed to find the edges of the little path quite easily in the dark and they ran along panting, trying to keep up with the speeding Angus.

Behind them came another howl, and then another, and this time the howls had a triumphant note as if the owners knew that at last they were on the trail of their quarry.

CHAPTER XX

The Magic Wood

GAVIN ran uphill, his heart pumping and his legs strangely stiff. As he ran, he could hear the howls of the dogs behind him and a swift glance over his shoulder told him that the dogs were racing down a hill on the other side of a little glen.

'Faster, faster!' called Angus, as he too looked back. Clare, Michael and Mot all set their minds to the task of running up the brae to where they could see the start of a wood about half-way up.

The terrifying howls grew louder and in backward glances they could now see the dogs had reached the foot of the hill.

The dogs paused for a moment and then saw their quarry further up. Both reared up on their hind legs and from their gaping mouths came terrible and fearsome snarls and bellows.

Then they fell back on all fours again, paused for an instant and with new bellows began to charge up the hill towards the children.

Gavin thought his lungs would burst. He was just behind Angus when he leapt into the trees and then halted, panting for breath. Clare, Michael and Mot crashed in behind them.

Before they could say anything, Angus ran to a little grove of trees.

'Rowans!' he cried. 'We're safe!' He snatched handfuls of leaves from a tree which had a kind of faint, white flower blossom on it.

'Quick!' he urged. 'All of you! Pick some of this!'

Without stopping to ask why, Clare, Gavin, Michael and Mot all did the same.

Suddenly Gavin let out a whoop of delight. 'Look!' he cried. 'Juniper!'

'Pull some up!' commanded Angus. 'There's no time to spare.' The children searched around and tugged up little bushes until they all had armfuls of rowan leaves and juniper.

'What now?' gasped Clare, trying to get her breath back.

'Keep close to me,' said Angus. 'All stand within touching distance of one another. They'll be on us soon. We must go to the edge of the wood because there will be other trees and plants which have good spirits in them which the dogs will fear.'

He tip-toed back to the edge of the trees and peered out. Just below, about half-way up the hill, the dogs had paused, sitting back on their haunches, with growls and snarls coming from their mouths and their red eyes glittering.

When they saw the children, they let out two more howls and then came racing uphill.

Just then, Gavin noticed a kind of thick moss at his feet. It stirred old memories about what Uncle Fergus had told him about plants and trees having good and bad spirits in them long ago.

He tugged at Angus's arm and pointed down silently.

Angus's face lit up. 'Fir club moss!' he said. 'That's one of the strongest good luck plants. Pick some of that too.'

Gavin gathered some handfuls and they followed Angus to the edge of the trees. They looked out. The dogs were just a few feet away, crouching down, snarling, ready to spring.

'Do what I do,' said Angus. He stepped out from the trees and brandished his rowan leaves, his juniper and his handfuls of fir club moss in front of the dogs.

'I don't like this one bit,' murmured Clare. 'But if we have to do it, we have to do it. Here's hoping it works.' She, too, stepped out.

Michael and Mot, for once lost for words, followed her. So did Gavin.

*When the dogs saw the children, they let out two more howls
and then came racing uphill.*

All of them waved their armfuls of leaves and plants and brandished them in front of the dogs. For good measure, Gavin also waved his staff.

The dogs reared up and then ran backwards and forwards as if they were trying to get through an invisible fence.

Their snarling and howling was blood-chilling and it was all the children could do not to drop everything and run.

Angus began to walk slowly towards the dogs. Fearing the worst, but remembering that Angus had said they should do everything he told them, the children did the same.

'If we survive this, then we'll survive anything,' muttered Gavin to Clare as they walked slowly forwards.

Meanwhile, Mot had accidentally dropped his plants and leaves, but had picked up all their staffs and he carried these in his arms. He was later to say that the bird carvings on the staffs and the new Cross had also helped.

The dogs continued to howl, but now they seemed puzzled and thwarted. They ran backwards and forwards, but came no nearer. Then, without warning, they turned and loped downhill and were soon lost from sight.

A faint howl from beyond the hill came back to the children, but it carried no note of menace. They were never to see the dogs again.

Clare sank down on the heather. 'That was close.'

'You can say that again,' said Michael

Mot, relieved now that the tension was over, said it again and Clare flung some heather at him. They were all laughing and joking now that the terrible dogs had gone.

Angus laughed too, but he stopped suddenly and said: 'We have to climb the hill now. You do not have much time for the ceremonies of the sacred fire. If you are late then twelve months will pass before the sacred ceremonies take place again.

'Come, follow me and—as always—do as I say.'

The children followed him uphill. As they were wending their way through steep boulders and rock pinnacles on the slopes of Ben Ledi, Clare turned to Gavin and said: 'That's another task completed. We were in the secret wood. I hadn't properly thought of that before.'

'Neither had I,' said Gavin. 'We were so busy with the dogs that I didn't think of that. Besides, I thought finding the juniper beside Loch Etive might be enough to count.'

He turned and told Michael and Mot what Clare had said and they gave a little cheer.

Angus, leading them uphill, turned round and asked them to be quiet. 'Save your breath for the climb,' he said. 'We must be on the summit before or just after the sun comes fully up.'

He looked very serious for a moment and said: 'This mountain is your last chance to get home. Follow me and do as I say in all things.'

Clare and the boys exchanged glances, and hurried uphill as the moonlight faded and the early light of the dawn began to break over the hills.

CHAPTER XXI

The Sacred Fire

'FIND a sheltered corner and sit down,' said Angus, as he led the way to a heap of boulders close to the top of the hill. There was now a strong wind which was also cold and the children were glad to huddle inside their plaids and to settle down behind stones.

'I have much to tell you,' said Angus. 'Hear me out in silence because you cannot return home without knowing this.'

Clare, Gavin, Michael and Mot looked at him in the half-dark and said nothing.

Angus went on: 'Ben Ledi is a sacred hill to the people who lived here long ago and it is still special to the people now. In the spring they send messengers to the top.

'They will be there, but you will not be able to see them, nor will they be able to see you. The lights you saw last night were from their houses and they put all of them out one by one in a sacred ceremony.'

Clare gave a little nod of understanding, and Angus went on: 'They light a fire on this hill and they cook a special bannock or scone and also a kind of sweet thick liquid, like a kind of custard.

'Now that we hear stories of a new Faith coming from the west they sometimes mark one of the bannocks with a little cross.'

This time Gavin nodded in understanding, followed by the others as they remembered what Naoise and Deirdre had told them.

Angus continued in his sing-song voice: 'They skip through

the embers of this fire and whoever gets the bannock with the special mark will have great good fortune in the next year.

'They split the scones and bannocks up and eat them, but they also throw pieces into the air as offerings to the birds and animals who might harm their flocks and herds, their cattle, goats and little sheep.'

He fell silent for a moment and Gavin said: 'Why do they do that, Angus? Why do they do that now, in the spring?'

'Yes,' said Clare. 'And why do we have to do it?'

'Hush,' said Angus with a smile. 'I will tell you everything. But first you have to light a fire on the summit. When you were climbing the hill I took some wood from a little grove of birches and took it uphill with me. Look!'

He pointed to the ground at his feet and there was a little pile of dead twigs. He gazed at it and his eyes glowed like fire. The astonished children saw the pile of dead twigs come alive and wriggle about and grow into branches and then go quiet and still once more.

'Take them,' said Angus, with a note of sadness in his voice. 'It is almost the last thing I will do for you. You have been good comrades for our short time together, and I will miss you.'

'Where are you going, Angus?' asked Gavin, saddened by the thought of losing their new friend.

'I cannot tell you that now,' said Angus. 'But my spirit will be here, on Ben Ledi, in the glens and straths of Balquhidder and Strathyre, on the mountains and beside the lochs. It will be here for those who have eyes to hear and ears to listen.

'But we have talked enough. Come now, we must act.'

He got to his feet, picked up the wood and stepped out into the wind on top of the mountain. He walked over to a large rock and placed the wood beside it.

'Give me all the plants and old feathers you have,' he said. 'You will need them no more.'

The children searched in their rucksacks and sporrans and

gave Angus all they had. He made a little pile beneath the branches and then took two stones from his sporran, struck them together and sparks flew out. A little flame appeared below the branches and soon they were burning steadily.

Angus was working with speed. He pulled out a little iron plate and put it over the fire. Then he placed dough and other materials on it and it began to harden and go brown. He marked one piece with a cross and then mixed them up.

The children sat silently, bewildered about what was going on.

'You must help me now,' said Angus. 'This is the Beltane ceremony, the start of the new year, when the sun comes in the spring and warm days of summer are not far off.

'When the people light their special fire on the hill, then down below all other fires are re-lit in the houses. Quick, you have now to carry out the special ceremonies.'

He looked round at them all. 'You must stand,' he said. He took a piece of the scone and handed it to Clare and said: 'Say this after me! This to you, oh wolf.' Clare repeated his words and Angus added: 'Fling the piece of food into the air and down the hill.' Clare did so and then sat down, her legs feeling a bit weak although she did not know why.

Angus handed another piece to Gavin and said: 'Say this after me. This to you, oh eagle.' Gavin, too, said: 'This to you, oh eagle,' and flung a piece of food down the hill.

Angus made Michael and Mot also stand up and say, in turn: 'This to thee, oh raven' and 'This to thee, oh hooded crow.' Then Angus himself added: 'This to thee, oh fox.'

He was silent for a moment and then turned to the children with a sad smile and said: 'It is finished. One of you had the marked piece. You will be safe now.'

They were all silent for a moment and then Clare said: 'How do you mean, Angus? How is it finished?'

The children all looked expectantly at him and there was

silence, broken only by the sighing of the wind and crackle of the wood in the little fire at their feet.

The sun became warm and golden and lit everything up, but before Angus could reply a little grey mist suddenly formed on a lower shoulder of the hill and then swirled around and grew bigger, sending long tendrils up on to the summit.

In a few seconds, bright sunlight became grey, swirling cloud. It was almost human, Gavin thought later, as it gathered around them like an embrace. They all looked at one another and then instinctively gathered together in a group.

Without thinking, Gavin put his hand out and held Clare's. Mot and Michael also huddled close.

The wind grew stronger and the mist grew thicker, but they were not afraid of it—why, they did not know.

'What do we do now, Clare?' asked Gavin as the wind began to batter them.

'I don't know,' said Clare. 'Hang on to me, though.'

The wind grew and grew and began to shriek, the mist swirled and rolled and they began to reel and stagger until they cried out in alarm. The last thing Gavin felt was Mot and Michael hanging on to his arm, he hanging on to them, Clare clutching at the strap of his sack—then the noise grew and grew, the mist swirled and eddied and they all felt as if they had been swept up on the wings of a giant bird.

They heard and felt the wind, as if in a giant storm. They saw and felt the grey mist. They sensed that they were soaring through the air—and then they knew nothing.

CHAPTER XXII

The Clan returns

CLARE sat up and rubbed her eyes. 'Where are we?' she asked.

She looked around in amazement. 'We're still on the summit of Ben Ledi,' she said. Sitting alongside her, looking bemused, were Gavin, Michael and Mot.

'Clare,' said the astounded Gavin. 'I think we're back home! We're still on Ben Ledi, but there's the concrete trig point on the top.' Then he looked down. 'And we're dressed differently!' he cried. 'Our plaids have gone. We're as we used to be.'

They all looked at one another.

'We're wearing the clothes we had on the day we were carried away,' said Michael. 'Look at us. We're the *same!* I'm sure of it.'

'Yes,' said Mot. 'I remember it all well.' He gazed around. 'And the hills are the same as they were. Look, there's Callander!'

Where he pointed they could see the sun glinting on the roofs of the town in the distance.

'The modern woods are back and the trees are different!' exclaimed Mot.

'Yes,' said Michael. 'It's exactly as we left it—there's the road and ... look, *cars* on it!'

They gazed around at the familiar landscape. Even as they spoke their adventures began to fade from their minds.

'We'd better go down,' said Clare. 'We'll be in enough trouble with Aunt Elspeth and Uncle Fergus for being out this long.'

Gavin thought for a moment. 'Em ... perhaps we won't be,'

he said. 'Perhaps the time now is exactly the same as when we left. The only problem is that they will think we've climbed Ben Ledi and we're not supposed to do that without telling Uncle Fergus or Aunt Elspeth where we're going.'

Clare agreed. 'Yes, I think it's probably the same time as when we left. Well ... we'll soon find out when we go down.'

'But what will we tell them?' asked Mot. 'If we tell them about Angus and the dogs and the witch, they'll just laugh.'

'True,' said Michael. 'I wonder if the antler is still there?'

'I don't think we'll experiment with that again,' muttered Clare—and then suddenly she had a thought.

'Look!' she said. 'The boulder is still there on the side of the hill. You can see it quite clearly against the waters of Loch Venacher.'

They all looked and easily spotted the large boulder down below, but this time it looked securely rooted.

'Oh, you know, I don't know what to think,' said Clare. 'It was some adventure, anyway.'

She added: 'We'd better go down and face the music now.'

They turned and trotted downhill, and as they neared the farm Clare said: 'We don't want to look silly, so leave the talking to me.'

'Are you sure that wouldn't *make* us look silly?' joked Mot, and he received a playful cuff on the ear from Clare.

When they reached the farm, Clare went on ahead and vanished inside for a moment. Then she came racing out:

'It's all right. It's the same day now as when it all happened. There's a calendar on the table and I've checked. There won't be too much of a fuss.'

They all trooped in silently, their minds still bemused by their adventures.

'Clare,' said Gavin. 'It surely wasn't all a dream.'

'No,' said Clare, slowly, 'Some kind of magic did happen. People long ago knew all about it. We were just lucky enough to stumble across it.'

'Or *un*lucky,' said Michael, remembering the dogs.

'Yes,' said Mot. 'But lots of it was good too.'

They sat down on seats in the hall of the farmhouse and were silent for a time, remembering Deirdre and Naoise, the special horn, the small dark men, the warriors of the Fianne, the terrible witch, and their new friend Angus.

'I know one thing,' said Clare.

'What's that?' asked Gavin.

'No one is to call me princess any more,' said Clare, rather embarrassed by the memory now they were home.

'Yes, oh Queen,' said Mot, and he received another cuff.

'Wait a moment,' said Gavin and vanished inside.

'Where's he off to?' asked Clare, puzzled. Gavin came back a few moments later and said quietly: 'The chest and the antler have both gone. There's nothing left. But at least I still have my notebook with the task written in it.'

He pulled it out and opened it at the page. 'There's nothing there!' he gasped. 'It's gone as well! Oh ... well, never mind. I can remember it.'

He tried to recite the tasks, but failed to remember them all.

The others tried too, but failed.

'It must be meant that we should forget,' said Clare. 'I'm finding it harder even now to remember all we did.'

'So am I,' said Mot, and Michael agreed. Their memories seemed to fade by the minute.

Aunt Elspeth suddenly called to them: 'Where have you lot been? I was expecting you for lunch and none of you turned up. Where were you? Not up to any mischief, I hope.'

Tactfully saying nothing about having been up Ben Ledi, they all went through for tea and passed the rest of the day in a kind of daze.

* * *

Later that evening Aunt Elspeth came into the back kitchen where the children were chatting and reading. She was carrying Clare's anorak in her hand.

'Clare!' she said. 'Tell me ... what on earth is this?'

She reached into Clare's pocket and pulled out a few scraps of oatmeal, the remains of Clare's dramach.

The children all looked at one another.

'Aunt Elspeth,' Clare said, winking at the others, 'I couldn't even begin to tell you .... '